FIRST BLOOD

AWAKENING SERIES BOOK 3

JANE HINCHEY

First Blood © 2017 Jane Hinchey

ACKNOWLEDGMENTS

Writing may be solitary but putting out a book is not. I'm blessed to have such amazing people help me on my author journey.

Alicia from iProofread and More - your fantastic editing makes me a better writer. Thank you.

Angela from Covered Creatively - your covers ROCK! Thank you.

To my readers group, Jane's Little Devils, you continue to be awesome. Really. You are amazing, each and every one of you. Thank you for loving what I do.

And finally – my family – thank you. None of this would be fun without your love and support.

He looked at her dead body at his feet, splayed out on her stomach, dark hair spread around her. The pool of blood seeped from beneath her in an ever-increasing circle. The demon who'd delivered her practically vibrated with glee.

"I found her." It grunted. If the demon had a tail, it would have been wagging.

"We'll see." He wedged his foot beneath her and rolled her onto her back. Her torso was shredded, a victim of the demon's claws. The coloring was right, the size and age right. Was it her? Crouching, he brushed the hair back from her face.

"Goddamn it!" he roared, rising to his feet, fists clenched. It wasn't her. Not her face and definitely no magic.

"Not her?" The demon bowed his head, dejected.

"Not her," he agreed. He wanted to punch his fist through the demon's chest and tear his heart out for his mistake. Instead, he clenched and released his fingers to curb the anger that pulsed through him. They were getting closer, he could feel it. For millennia Zachariah had been his target, yet he'd eluded him. For all these years he'd remained invisible to him, out of reach, untouchable. And all these years he'd searched, the prophecy breathing down his neck. It had to be stopped. For she was the most powerful witch ever created, and her unborn child even more so. She had the power that he needed, the magic that he would steal not only from her, but all the witches, and infuse it into his Nephilim army, to make them invincible. He had to steal her power before she used it against him. The easiest way to do that? Kill her.

Crossing to the ancient bowl set upon a pedestal, he waved his hand over the black liquid within, a smirk curling his lips as the water rippled. Closing his eyes, he sucked in a deep breath, releasing it as he held both hands above the liquid, feeling the connection, the energy transfer from the black depths to him and back again.

Opening his eyes, he leaned over and peered into the inky darkness, the ripples smoothing away until he could see the image clearly, playing out like a movie.

WHERE IS she and how did she get here? Confused, Georgia looks over her shoulder. Nothing. The streetlights are out the houses on either side of the road dark. It's pitch black, silent, and eerie. The wind suddenly gusts, blowing her loose hair around her head. She reaches up to brush it out of her eyes, shivering, rubbing her hands up and down her arms.

"Zak!" she calls, startled to hear her own voice echo back at her. Echo? In the middle of a street? What the hell is going on? Out of the corner of her eye, she sees something and swivels, wincing as the asphalt digs into her bare feet. A mist is rolling in, a big gray wave that appears bigger and bigger, slowly creeping toward her, obscuring everything in its path. Something tells her the fog is not a good thing.

Turning, she runs, yet she gets nowhere, makes no progress. The street is endless, no twists or turns, just more straight road ahead of her. Her feet are stinging and her heart pumping as she glances over her shoulder. The fog is closer now, almost upon her. Panic spikes, adrenaline fuelling her, she pushes harder. Must. Get. Away.

Then it's upon her, the gray surrounds her, swallows her whole and she staggers to a halt, unable to see a foot in front of her. It's cold. Deathly cold. A hand clamps down on her shoulder and she screams, spinning.

"You're going the wrong way," Dainton tells her, his eyes empty, devoid of emotion.

"Dainton? What are you doing here? Where are we? And what do you mean, going the wrong way?" But he's not looking at her; he's looking over her head. She casts a glance over her shoulder, but she can't see what he's looking at. What can he see that she can't?

"Dainton? Come on, you're scaring me." He doesn't answer, just brushes past her, bumping her with his shoulder. She staggers, regains her balance in time to see his back disappear into the fog.

"Dainton! Come back! Wait!" She takes off after him, but he's gone, swallowed up by the fog. Stopping, she holds her breath, listening. Not a sound. Not even his footsteps. But now she's all turned around. He said she was going the wrong way, but which way was that? She couldn't see a damn thing and it's freezing here. Maybe she'd try and find a house, bang on the door until they let her in. They could call Zak to come get her. Nodding her head she begins walking again, but no matter what direction she tries, nothing changes. The road remains beneath her feet, sharp and painful. She can't find the footpath, let alone a house.

Calling upon her magic, she creates a ball of light, holding it in front of her to illuminate the way. Then she hears it.

Faint at first. Pausing, she listens. What is that? A whooshing noise. Getting louder. Closer. Is it coming toward her or is she traveling toward it? She can't tell. Her chest tightens, panic dancing across her skin. WHOOSH! A giant wing brushes past her face, knocking her backward. She trips and falls, elbows scraping painfully on the bitumen.

"Who's there?" she demands, crouching, ignoring her stinging elbows. Someone is playing with her, taunting her, and her fear is slowly being replaced with anger. Do they even know who they're messing with? She has the power of a thousand witches within her. She'll singe his sorry feathers until they're nothing but stumps.

WHACK! A wing clips her across the back of her head and she tumbles forward, this time her knees taking the brunt. Goddamn it, she'd be grazed all over at this rate!

"Show yourself, coward!" she demands, climbing to her feet, ignoring the trickle of blood she could feel running down her shins. Then she sees it, coming toward her through the mist. Big. Giant. Massive. A being with the biggest wings she'd ever seen. She squints. What is that? The shape looks like a man, but it's dark, she can't make out his features, and he is twice the size of a normal man. What is he? Not angel, too big, too evil, for she could feel it oozing from him in waves, lapping at her, repulsing her. The wings had to span at least twenty feet each, and as he gets closer, he grows larger. A giant. Turning, she runs. She feels the wind buffet her as he moves his wing, getting ready to strike. If he hits her, she'll die. She knows it, senses it. So she runs, ignoring her shredded feet, bleeding knees, and elbows. She runs for her life.

"Georgia!" Her cheek stung and she blinked, sucking in a startled breath.

"Zak?" Confused, she looked up into the face of her fiancé. His dark eyes stared back at her, full of concern.

4

Gently he cupped her cheek, his fingers soothing her stinging flesh and she sighed.

"What are you doing?" she murmured, thankful to be tucked up warm in bed.

"You were dreaming. I couldn't wake you, so I slapped you. Sorry."

"You slapped me!" She sat up, outraged, then saw the blood on the sheets. Throwing the covers off, she looked at her dirty feet: blood smeared everywhere. Her knees and elbows, while healed, were still covered in blood.

"You were hurt. Bleeding. Thrashing about and calling for Dainton."

"Just a really vivid dream," she reassured Zak, sliding from the bed. She needed to get cleaned up.

"You don't bleed in dreams," he pointed out, climbing out of bed and standing with his hands on his hips.

"No. You don't," she agreed. She didn't know what to tell him. The truth? That some sort of giant creature with massive wings had been trying to kill her? And that Dainton had been there to warn her. "But I'm not exactly normal. I'm sure it's okay," she lied, placing a hand on his arm to soothe him. "Nothing to worry about."

Of course, he didn't believe her. The way his brow arched and his head tilted told her that much.

2

The blob of gel on her stomach was cold and Georgia sucked in a startled breath. The technician looked at her and grinned.

"Sorry, should have warned you that would be a little cold."

"That's okay." Georgia shrugged and Zak clasped her hand, wrapping her fingers tight in his. He was nervous and it was adorable. They hadn't spoken any more about her nightmare. She'd cleaned up, he'd made her a hot chocolate, then they'd climbed back into bed and talked about today, what they hoped would happen until she'd drifted off to sleep in his arms.

"Here we go. I'm going to move the transducer over your stomach now." The technician smiled a big bright smile and began pushing a handheld device over her abdomen. They were about to see their baby for the first time and couldn't wait. They both looked at the screen in anticipation, but couldn't make out anything from the black and gray image. It looked a lot like a sonar of the ocean floor.

"Hmmm." The technician muttered beneath her breath,

pressing a little harder, moving the roller up and down, from side to side.

"Is something wrong?" Georgia asked. But she already knew. She looked at Zak who was already shaking his head in resignation, his fingers squeezing hers in an almost bone-crushing grip.

"I'm so sorry, Ms. Pearce. Georgia." The technician glanced at the screen to read her name. "But there's no heartbeat. In fact—there's no baby." Her voice had taken on that professional tone when delivering bad news, gone was the jovial technician from minutes earlier.

"I can't believe Jelly Bean is doing this to us. Again." Georgia shook her head, giving Zak a small grin.

"She does want to stay hidden," he agreed. They'd been to a handful of medical appointments to monitor Georgia's pregnancy and all had been the same—besides her swollen abdomen, there was no medical indication she was pregnant. Jelly Bean, as they'd nicknamed her, was using magic to block them. She kicked now and Georgia pressed Zak's hand to where the little foot could be clearly seen pressing against her skin.

"I get the feeling she's going to be quite a handful." He chuckled. "Like her mother."

"She sure is! I can't wait to meet her."

"Ummm." The technician frowned at them, clearly confused, "I'm going to get my supervisor to come in and take a look. It could be a fault in the machine."

"Your machine is fine." Zak sighed, handing Georgia a towel to wipe the gel from her stomach.

"How many weeks are you?" The technician asked, eyeing Georgia's belly. She couldn't see the baby moving, little limbs poking and stretching the skin in certain places before settling into a different position.

"Around thirty-five weeks. Don't worry, this has

happened before," Georgia reassured the technician who was looking at them as if they were crazy. "I'm a witch and my baby is too. She's cloaking herself."

"She? Witch?" The technician squeaked, finally letting go of the transducer, the sound of it dropping into its slot on the machine loud in the small dim room.

"I get a sense this little one is a girl." Georgia lovingly caressed her baby bump.

"Ma'am, I'm really sorry, but there is no baby. My best guess is that whatever is distending your stomach like that is fluid buildup. You need urgent medical attention."

"It's not fluid buildup, it's not a tumor or a growth, and I'm not crazy." Georgia sighed, sitting up and maneuvering herself to the edge of the examination table. "Babe, you'd better do your thing before she starts a panic," she told Zak.

"On it." The technician looked at him in alarm as he approached and placed his hands on her shoulders, leaned forward and stared intently into her eyes.

"We weren't here. This never happened. You will delete all mention of Georgia Pearce from your system. You will forget this conversation. Understood?"

"Understood." The technician's pupils expanded then dilated as Zak's compulsion altered her perception of reality. Turning to the machine, she began typing, Zak watching over her shoulder as she deleted Georgia's information from the system.

Sliding from the table, Georgia pulled her T-shirt down and her maternity jeans up. It had been worth a shot and she was disappointed it hadn't worked—like any expectant mother she wanted reassurance that her baby was okay, that she was developing properly. And it would be nice to have a definitive due date. Georgia had none of that, and given she was a witch-vampire hybrid, who knew how long her pregnancy would last? All she had to go on was her human experiences and that told her forty weeks was the norm.

"Ready?" Linking his fingers with hers, Zak smiled down at her.

"Ready." She nodded.

Outside they stood by her red antique Ford Jailbar truck. She loved this truck, had found it in her old barn when she was renovating her farmhouse and had it fully restored. Trouble was it was a two-seater cab and soon they'd be a family of three. No room for a baby seat.

"I promised Mrs. Montanari I'd drop in, help her with her garden." She spoke to Zak over the hood as she headed for the driver's side.

"Aston said he had something he needed to show me. I'll meet you later back home?"

"After Mrs. Montanari, I'm meeting Skye for dinner and then the coven has a meeting, so I'll be a while."

"Don't overdo it," Zak warned, coming around the truck, tilting her face up to his and lowering his mouth to hers. Wrapping her arms around his neck, she leaned into his kiss, the heat sizzling between them as he nudged her back against the truck and nestled himself against her.

"You undo me," he muttered, tearing his mouth away, breathing hard.

"You complete me." She grinned, cupping his ass through his denim jeans.

"Marry me then," he grumbled, swatting her hands away.

"I told you after the baby is born. I am not getting married while I'm knocked up."

"Are you sure you're not using that as an excuse? Stalling?" She could tell he was concerned, that he was worried she had cold feet.

"Babe, if I didn't want to marry you I wouldn't be wearing this!" She waved her hand in the air, the sunlight glinting off the diamond on her left hand. "I love you, and our baby, more than anything—and I can't wait to start our lives together. But I want to enjoy each moment as it comes. Right now, baby comes first and I just want to bask in it, not be distracted by the countless decisions that come with planning a wedding." Tugging his head back down to hers, she whispered against his lips, "Be patient with me. Please."

Groaning, he opened his mouth to her, his tongue dueling with hers and his hands reaching for hers again and planting her palms against his ass. She smiled against his lips.

"I want you so damn much," he muttered, the evidence clear as he pressed against her.

"Me too," she whimpered in return, her knees turning to jelly. A car tooting its horn brought them both back to reality with a jolt. Grinning ruefully, he eased back, putting some space between them.

"I'll see you back home later. Call me if you need me." He dropped a quick hard kiss on her lips, strode into the alley by the side of the medical building, and teleported. With a sigh Georgia straightened from where she was leaning against the truck and opened the door, pulling herself up and in behind the wheel.

3

"What seems to be the problem, Mrs. Montanari?" Georgia followed the elderly woman through her small cottage and out into the back garden.

"It's my vegetable garden," Mrs. Montanari said sadly. "I've tried everything. Fertilizers, pellets, sprays, mulch. I've had the radio on playing classical music. I talk to them. Nothing is working." She shuffled down the garden path, dodging stacks of empty pots and bags of potting mix.

"So they aren't growing?" Georgia pressed, admiring the beautiful flowers and fruit trees she passed. Mrs. Montanari's garden was wonderful, a lovingly tended chaotic mess.

"Not only aren't they growing, they're dying. It's like the vegetable plot is cursed. My carrots, potatoes, tomatoes, cabbages. All dead. Everything I plant here dies. I don't understand it." She wrung her hands, agitated, anxiety tinting her cheeks pink.

"Don't worry, we'll get to the bottom of it," Georgia assured her, coming to stand next to her as they both gazed at the sorry-looking vegetable plot. Mrs. Montanari was right: something was off here. The rest of her garden was lush and green. Although not immaculate in layout or composition, it was healthy. The vegetable patch, on the other hand, was brown, wilted. And from where Georgia was standing the dark energy was palpable.

"Tell me, Mrs. Montanari, is there anyone who wouldn't want your vegetable garden to flourish?" she asked. She suspected a hex was in play here. Leaning down she held her hand over the soil, searching for traces of poisons or toxins. Nope. The garden hadn't been poisoned in the traditional sense.

"I guess anyone who's entering the pumpkin-growing competition this year." Mrs. Montanari shrugged. "I've won three years in a row. I know some people are upset about that."

"Hmmm. Okay." Georgia glanced down at the plump figure of Mrs. Montanari, grinning at her ensemble of crocks with socks, a floral housedress, apron, and big straw hat, strands of gray hair poking out.

"I'm going to need your help," Georgia told her. Mrs. Montanari nodded so hard her hat almost fell off.

"Anything, my dear, anything. What do you need me to do?"

"Hold my hands, and I need you to say these words with me. Do you think you can do that?"

"Of course! But what is it we're doing?"

"I think someone has hexed your garden. We're going to fight darkness with light and protect not only your garden but also you and your house," Georgia explained.

"Oh, that sounds wonderful."

"Turn to face me. Now hold both of my hands in yours." They stood facing each other, hands clasped.

"Do I need to close my eyes?" Mrs. Montanari asked.

"Only if you want to. It's not necessary. Okay, take a deep breath in, fill your lungs all the way, then slowly blow it out.

We'll do this three times. Then I want you to repeat what I say, and we'll do that three times as well. Ready? Breathe."

They stood together at the foot of the vegetable garden, breathing in deep breaths.

"*Contego, servo, vindico, protego.*" Georgia spoke out loud and Mrs. Montanari repeated the words. As they continued to chant, the plants in the garden bed started to move, to stand up tall, turn green and grow. Blossoms appeared. After the final round, Georgia released Mrs. Montanari's hands and looked at the older woman who stood with her eyes closed, her face screwed up in concentration.

"Open your eyes, Mrs. Montanari, and look at your garden."

Mrs. Montanari blinked, her hands covering her mouth in shock before dropping to her sides, her face beaming.

"My garden! It's beautiful! Oh, my goodness, thank you, thank you, thank you!" She wrapped Georgia in a hug, patting her baby bump and telling Jelly Bean she had a very clever mommy.

"What do I owe you?" she asked, practically skipping ahead of Georgia on the path back to the cottage.

"Nothing at all. It was my pleasure. You shouldn't have any more trouble now, but let me know if you have any problems, okay?"

"Thank you, my dear, you are a wonderful soul. Oh, before you go, I have this for you." She rushed over to the sofa where a brown paper bag sat. Picking it up, she handed it to Georgia. Inside was a crocheted baby blanket in a rainbow of pastel colors.

"It's beautiful! Thank you so much. You didn't have to do this," Georgia said, touched by Mrs. Montanari's gesture.

"Nonsense. You've always had time for me, my child. Half of my furniture is from your shop. It's nice to be able to do something for you. I know you don't have your mama and papa to celebrate the birth of your baby, so I figured this doddery old woman could at least make you a blanket."

Eyes tearing up, Georgia hugged her. It meant the world to her that Mrs. Montanari had made the blanket for her and her baby. And she was right—the only family Georgia had left was her sister, Skye, and she was pretty sure, while Skye would buy wonderful gifts for the baby, anything handmade was not on the cards.

"It's beautiful. I'll treasure it always." Wiping away a stray tear, she smiled again at Mrs. Montanari and said her goodbyes.

"You going to finish that?" Georgia eyed the half-eaten burger on Skye's plate. Skye laughed. "Go ahead."

Snatching the burger up, Georgia took a bite, her cheeks bulging. Ever since she'd turned into a witch, her appetite for food had returned, negating her need for blood. Skye, on the other hand, didn't need food to survive. Ever since Zak turned her into a vampire to save her life, blood was what she needed. Georgia knew her sister had ordered the burger so that Georgia wasn't eating alone and she appreciated her sacrifice. Food sat heavily in a vampire's stomach, not a pleasant sensation.

Gulping the burger down in record time, Georgia wiped her face with a napkin before glancing at the time on her phone.

"Shit. I need to go get Carol. I said I'd give her a lift." Pushing back her chair, she struggled to her feet, her belly large in front of her. Of course, ever since she'd gotten knocked up her appetite had increased tenfold, and she was constantly hungry.

"I can go pick her up if you like?" Skye offered, reaching out a hand to help her.

"I've got this. I'm pregnant, not an invalid," Georgia grumbled, shooing her away. Skye bit back a smile. They'd all been treating Georgia with kid gloves and it was driving her mad.

"Can you go to the farmhouse, let the others know I'm running late?" Georgia asked.

"Sure, no problem." Skye matched her steps to Georgia's as they made their way outside. The sun was setting on the horizon, painting the sky in a vibrant shade of orange. It was the night of their weekly coven meeting.

It felt like yesterday when her Aunt Melissa had turned up on their doorstep and announced she was a witch and had started to train Georgia and Skye in the art of witchcraft. Her Aunt's betrayal, trying to drain her of her magic and use her power to kill the Witch Hunter had backfired. The Hunter was one step ahead, as always. He'd killed Georgia, effectively killing the coven of witches she was linked too, including her Aunt. But Georgia wasn't dead, simply in a different dimension, and using her bond with Zak she'd found her way back. She'd killed the Hunter, freeing the magic of the hundreds of witches that he'd killed and now had more magic coursing through her veins than she knew what to do with, for she'd absorbed *all* of the witches' magic.

Then, she'd discovered she was pregnant. It was the Hunters dying words to her. That inside her womb she carried the next generation of witches, a very powerful new breed of witch. That's when Georgia had embraced witchcraft wholeheartedly, to fulfill the legacy growing within her. She'd decided to rebuild her Aunt's coven, to make it her own, a safe space for her and her baby. The new generation of witches. Besides her and Skye, there were another eight witches, and while Skye's magic hadn't come in—most likely due to her being a vampire—she helped Georgia with running the coven and keeping the witches organized.

Stopping by her truck, Georgia dug around in her pocket for the keys and unlocked the door, giving Skye a look over her shoulder.

"Do not even think of offering to help me get in my own truck or so help me God I will zap you."

Skye laughed, backing up a couple of steps. "Okay, okay, little Miss Independent. Have it your way. But I will stand here and laugh at your attempts to haul your pregnant ass into that truck."

Grabbing the steering wheel with one hand and the overhead handle in the other, Georgia grunted and puffed as she maneuvered herself up and into the cab. She blew out a breath and wiped at the perspiration on her face, then eyed Skye again. "I'm in. Now go. I'll swing by and pick up Carol and will be out at the farm in about half an hour or so."

Gunning the engine she peeled out of the parking lot, the radio blasting as it always did. She'd miss this. Once bubs arrived there'd be no more drives in her candy apple red truck. Zak had already bought her a red Cherokee Jeep, baby seat installed and ready to go. It sat in the newly built garage at his house, un-driven.

Georgia drove through the streets of Redmeadows singing along to the Luke Bryan song on the radio, thrumming her fingers on the steering wheel. The baby kicked and she laughed. "You like this music, Bubba?" she murmured to her bump. "Good taste, baby, good taste."

Turning into Carol's street, she slowed to a stop at the curb out front of the red brick townhouse where she lived. *That's odd.* There was no sign of Carol. She'd expected her to be waiting impatiently by the curb. Frowning, Georgia thought back. Had she got the message wrong? She'd thought it was today's meeting that Carol had needed a lift to since her car was being serviced. Maybe she'd gotten it wrong. Apparently, baby brain really was a thing.

Georgia parked her truck and slid out, tugging her maternity T-shirt down over her bump. She loved her denim maternity jeans but frowned at her feet, so swollen all she could wear were flip flops and not her beloved boots.

Pulling her phone out of her back pocket, she dialed Carol's number as she walked up the front path. She was climbing the front steps when she heard it. The phone ringing inside Carol's townhouse...the front door standing open. Halting at the top of the steps, Georgia pushed out her senses, searching for Carol and anything else that might have been in the vicinity. Nothing. She got nothing.

"Carol?" Stepping closer to the front door, she peered into the darkness. Carol wouldn't have gone out and left her front door open. And she wouldn't have left her phone behind either. What was going on?

Heart thumping in her chest, Georgia stepped over the threshold and felt along the wall for the light switch. She flicked it on and blinked, adjusting to the beam of light.

"Oh no," she whispered. The room was a mess. Furniture tipped over, pictures shaken loose from the wall. But no Carol. Using her senses again, Georgia felt for her. Nope, definitely not here, but not dead—she could feel that she was still on this plane, just not at this location. Closing her eyes, she concentrated, using her magic and her senses to try and see what had happened here, but she hit an invisible wall. Something was blocking her, but what she did pick up sent a slither up her spine. Was that...demon? How could that be possible when Zak had destroyed them all in Eden Hills? Had they regrouped?

Thumb hitting a familiar button on her screen, she put the phone to her ear.

"What's up, gorgeous?" Zak's deep voice was crystal clear through the speaker as if he were standing next to her.

"I just swung by to pick up Carol and she's not here," Georgia explained.

"She probably caught a lift with one of the other witches." She could imagine him shrugging, unconcerned.

"No, I mean, she's been taken. There are signs of a struggle. And, Zak? I swear I can sense demon here."

"Not possible!" That got his attention.

"Afraid so. I need you to come."

"Get out of there. Immediately. I'm on my way." A moment's pause, then "Fuck. I haven't been to Carol's before. What's the street name again?"

"Talbot." Backing out of the doorway, Georgia carefully made her way down the stairs and out on the front footpath to wait for Zak. He'd teleport here within seconds, but he could only teleport to places he'd been before, and he'd never been to Carol's house, but he'd made the effort to tour almost every street in Redmeadows and memorize them for future use.

Sure enough, he appeared moments later fifty yards down the street from where Georgia was standing.

"Are you all right?" Zak rushed to her, his hand sliding over her baby bump as he peered into her eyes.

"I'm totally fine, stop fussing. Go in there and tell me you can trace the demon who took her."

"Kiss first," he demanded and she couldn't help the grin that pulled at her lips. Despite being eight months pregnant she constantly wanted this man. It seemed her libido was as ferocious as her food appetite.

"No time for fooling around, Goodwin." She offered up a peck on his lips then pulled away, knowing if she lingered they'd end up rolling around on the front lawn disgracing themselves. It had happened before and she'd been mortified.

Leaning in close, he pressed his lips to her forehead. "Wait here. I mean it, don't come inside."

"Fine." Cradling her baby bump Georgia waited. She'd already done what she could anyway, maybe Zak would find something she'd missed. Cursing beneath her breath and worried for her friend, she satisfied herself with pacing along the footpath until Zak returned.

"Well?" she demanded.

"Sweetheart, you've been under a lot of pressure lately." He put an arm around her shoulders and turned her away from the townhouse, urging her toward her truck.

"What do you mean? What did you find?"

"Not a whole lot. And certainly no demon."

"What are you talking about? I felt traces of demon, I'm certain of it."

"I think your pregnancy hormones are throwing things off balance, babe. No demons."

Stopping at her truck Georgia eyed him. "Are you saying I imagined it?"

Grinning at her narrowed eyes and hands-on-hip stance, he shook his head. "Nope, I'm saying pregnancy may have caused your senses to go on the fritz. Come on, hop in, I'll drive you home."

"No. We can't leave. We have to report this."

"What, to Rhys?" Zak sniggered. Rhys, her werewolf best friend, had dropped off the radar a couple of months ago, no longer returning phone calls or messages, and when Georgia had turned up at the police station to confront him she'd been stunned to hear he was on extended leave. She assumed it was pack related. After all, when the Hunter had killed his Alpha Hayden and the Alpha's wife Alison last year in an attempt to get Georgia and her Aunt, Rhys had been fast-tracked into stepping up into the role of Alpha.

She'd been friends with Rhys since they were kids, he'd

stuck by her when Zak had turned her into a vampire, even though he didn't like it, he didn't give up on her. She worried now that involving him in her run from the Hunter had been too much, for she still felt it was her fault the plane had crashed, killing Hayden and Alison and their unborn child. The mere thought of it tore her up inside and she wished Rhys would talk to her about it, but he'd pulled away. She could only hope that after time they could repair their friendship.

"To the police. It's still a crime scene, and even though Carol is a witch, she's human too. Hasn't there been a spate of human disappearances lately? We have to assume it's the same person who's doing this, kidnapping witches and humans. Maybe they've mistaken the humans for witches, who knows, but I'm not just walking away and leaving Carol's house like this." She huffed, annoyed at Zak's dig about Rhys and worried for her friend.

Blowing out a resigned sigh, Zak nodded. "Fine. Call the cops."

"THANKS FOR YOUR HELP, Georgia. I'm sorry about your friend." Constable Brey Woods snapped closed his notebook and gave her a tired smile.

"I hope you find her. And the others." Georgia shifted her weight from foot to foot, her back aching at having to stand around for the last hour while the police inspected Carol's townhouse and then interviewed her.

"Have you heard from Rhys at all?" she asked, knowing it was a long shot. She heard Zak's snort and shot him a glance. He was leaning against her truck, waiting impatiently for her to finish.

"No, ma'am. Sorry. You know he's taken twelve months leave though, right?"

"Yes. They told me. It's just that I can't get hold of him, and with everything that's going on, I can't help but be worried. Could he have been taken?"

"I'm sure it would have been reported if he was missing. Now that he lives out of town it's unlikely he's been caught up in this. So far the perpetrator has targeted homes within Redmeadows itself."

"Well, if you do hear from him, Brey, would you ask him to call or text me? Please."

"Sure thing, ma'am. You have a good night now."

"Goodnight." Turning away she walked toward Zak, who straightened and stepped forward, wrapping an arm around her shoulders. "You're cold," he muttered.

It was true, a shiver danced over her skin, but it wasn't from the cold. Something wasn't right. Frowning, she let him help her into the passenger side of her truck. He pulled the seatbelt over her extended abdomen and stole a kiss.

"You know I love you, right?" he whispered, his lips a hairsbreadth from hers.

"I love you too, but I can't—"

"Shh." He placed a finger over her lips, hushing her. "Humor me, will you? I'll get the boys over to investigate Carol's disappearance." Looking into his dark eyes, she relented.

"Let's go home." She knew what was coming. He was going to ask her to stop looking for her witch, to leave it to him and his warriors. But she couldn't do that.

"So if it wasn't demon in there, what was it?" she asked, settling back into the seat as Zak started the truck and smoothly pulled away.

"Vampire. But not recent. A very old, very faint trace of vampire, so I don't think it was a vampire that took her. I didn't get the sense of any other paranormal, so I'm thinking your kidnapper is human. He's not targeting witches, he's targeting women."

"I still don't understand how you couldn't sense the demon." Georgia twisted her hands in her lap.

"Because there wasn't one there, love." Zak patted her hands, stilling them. "Don't upset yourself over it. I'll get the boys over here as soon as the police have cleared out. We should be able to track her."

Georgia lapsed into silence. Six weeks ago the first woman had gone missing, taken from her home at night. Two weeks after that the same thing had happened to another human. And now, two weeks later, Carol. It was puzzling the police hadn't caught the person responsible yet. And to be honest, Georgia thought Zak and his warriors could have acted faster at catching the guy too. Were they all too distracted with the impending arrival of the baby that they weren't taking any of this seriously?

Lost in thought she was unprepared for the vision that appeared out of nowhere. It was Zak, standing with his warriors, and behind him, Veronica, the vampire who'd betrayed Zak and who Georgia had ultimately killed, and a house Georgia had never seen before. She could smell sulfur and wrinkled her nose. Then she saw them. Dozens upon dozens of demons, their black skin gleaming in the moon-light, their red eyes glowing. She shivered. They were running at Zak when he raised his hands and a blast shook the earth and the demons fell. All of them gone, nothing but ash falling atop the ruins of the house. Georgia realized this was his house that had been razed in Eden Hills before they'd even met. Why was she seeing a vision of it now? And Zak's eyes—they glowed green from the power he'd just unleashed.

Zak and his warriors gathered around looking at the ring on his hand—Georgia knew without a doubt that the red strand around the ring had started to glow. This was when the ring and dagger had first been activated, back when she'd first discovered the dagger hidden in the wall of her workshop, how she'd cut her finger on the blade pulling it from its hiding place, triggering the connection between Zak's ring and the dagger itself. That's how he found her, once the connection between ring and dagger had been established he just had to follow the trail, leading him to her doorstep.

What had followed had changed her life forever, for they'd discovered her dagger had the power to bring death to immortals, and Zak's ring could restore life to immortals. His ring had been used to resurrect an ancient original vampire, Marius, who in turn had drained Skye dry and left her for dead, and kidnapped Georgia.

Moving her attention away from the warriors gathered around Zak and frowning at the ring, she looked at the wreck of Zak's house and that's when she saw him. At least she thought it was a male, it was hard to tell, but there in the shadows, a dark figure. Not a demon. His head lifted and he looked directly at her, his black eyes turning to red, his wings stretching out on either side of him, first white, then red, dripping in blood. At his feet, dead bodies. Not of demons, but humans. With a flap of his wings, the vision ended.

Sucking in a startled gasp, her hand at her throat, Georgia blinked, her vision clearing.

"What? What is it? Is it the baby?" Zak pulled over with a screech of tires.

"No. The baby is fine. I had a vision."

"A vision? Of what?"

"I think I just saw the day the demons destroyed your home in Eden Hills." Another shudder ran through her. Who was this dark angel? And what did the vision mean? Was he responsible for the missing witches? Was the vision a sign he was coming for her? He'd looked straight at her as if he could see her, and the cruel twist of his lips made her blood run cold.

"Fuck this. I'm getting you home." Zak swore, reaching for her, but she pressed back against the door, out of his reach.

"No! No teleporting, Zak. I'm not risking the baby."

"Damn it, Georgia." Zak slammed his hand down on the steering wheel.

"Hey! Take it easy on my car," she scolded, reaching out to place a calming hand on his arm. "Drive me home. It was just a vision. I'm not in danger."

After a moment's silence, he nodded. "Very well."

4

Pulling up outside his house, Zak helped her down from her truck and inside. The warriors and Skye were waiting, hovering around her.

"For goodness sake, guys!" Georgia snapped. "Chill out. I'm fine. The baby's fine. Nothing bad happened to me. If only you shared the same concern for Carol!"

"Wait for me in the front room." Zak addressed them and they all dutifully scurried away. Except for Skye, who refused to leave her sister's side.

"I'm fine, honestly," Georgia grumbled, missing the look that passed between Skye and Zak.

"Sit." Zak settled her in an armchair, lifting her feet and sliding an ottoman beneath them. In the kitchen he placed a heat bag in the microwave, waiting impatiently for it to finish heating before returning and tucking it against her lower back.

"I'll take the warriors out tonight, put an end to these abductions once and for all."

"Thank you."

"I know you think we haven't been trying, but the warriors have been out every night patrolling."

"I'm sorry I snapped. I know you're all trying to help. I'm worried we've got another Hunter on our hands," Georgia admitted. "Who's to say there wasn't another awakening triggered after the Hunter was killed? I mean the prophecy of me and my baby is huge. There have to be others that will try and stop us."

"I think your imagination is running away with you." Zak dismissed her concerns with a wave of his hand. "Initially I thought we could be dealing with a rogue vampire, but now I'm starting to think it's a depraved human we should be searching for."

"Go. Go meet with your warriors." Georgia waved him away, leaning back against the chair and closing her eyes. Lord, she was tired. Growing another human was exhausting.

"Do the others in the coven know about Carol?" she asked Skye, eyes still closed.

"No, but they knew something was up when you called to cancel."

"Can you check in on them, make sure they all got home safely?"

"Sure." Pulling out her phone, Skye paced the room as she made the calls. Georgia listened, lightly dozing, only opening her eyes when Zak crouched by her side.

"We're heading out, babe. You okay here?"

"I'm heading up to bed in a little bit, once Skye has checked in on my coven and made sure they all made it home safe and sound."

"I can wait," he offered, running his fingers across her cheek in a whisper-soft caress.

"No, you go, hunt down this bastard and get my witch

back. I'm fine. I've got Skye here to take care of me. Not that I need taking care of."

Zak laughed, rising to his feet. "Call me if you need me." Then his warriors gathered around him, Hands on each other's shoulders, they disappeared in the blink of an eye.

"Sorry, you're stuck babysitting me." Georgia scowled. She'd had someone with her almost constantly since she discovered she was pregnant, and it grated on her nerves. She liked her space, needed her space. To have them hovering around her irritated her beyond belief. Plus she didn't need protecting. She had so much magic at her disposal it was *she* who should be protecting all of *them*!

When Georgia struggled to get up out of the armchair, Skye stood, arms crossed, watching her. They were right. She couldn't even get her fat ass out of a chair. She flopped back, tears filling her eyes.

"Oh hey." Skye rushed to her side, clasping her hand. "It's okay."

"It's not. Look at me. I'm huge. I can't even stand up on my own. My back hurts. My ribs hurt. My feet ache. I have to pee every two minutes." Yeah, the downside of having all this magic was she couldn't use it to make her advanced state of pregnancy comfortable.

"You're missing something." Skye pulled her to her feet. "You're glowing, you're radiant and what you're doing, having this baby is a miracle. You're a goddess."

"Pft." Wiping an arm over her damp eyes, Georgia waddled across the room. "I'm going to pee. You don't need to follow me."

"I'll wait here. Call out if you need anything."

Ten minutes later Georgia returned and eased herself back into the armchair. Skye was stretched out on the sofa, slim legs encased in denim and looking impossibly long.

Georgia scowled. She felt fat, ugly and unattractive in comparison.

"Tell me what happened at Carol's. Do you really think a human is behind this?" Skye asked.

Georgia shook her head. "I do not. When I went into Carol's home I sensed demon, yet Zak couldn't. But I swear, Skye, a demon had been in Carol's house. Recently. And then driving home, I had a vision of when the demons attacked Zak's house in Eden Hills, and their energy was the same as what I felt in Carol's place. And I saw something else. A dark angel. His wings were dripping blood and bodies were piled at his feet."

"Do you want me to get the grimoires? See if we can find anything about these demons?" What Georgia hadn't told Skye, hadn't told anyone, was that she didn't need the grimoires. When she'd absorbed the magic of hundreds of witches she'd absorbed their knowledge; there was nothing new the grimoires could teach her. But to keep Skye involved, to make her feel a part of the Coven, Georgia nodded.

"Yes, please."

Skye bounded upstairs to Georgia and Zak's room where she'd stacked the grimoires on the floor. Ten in all. Coming back downstairs, Skye cradled three grimoires in her arms, the old leather-bound tombs huge.

"Let's start with these." Dropping them onto the coffee table with a thump, she handed the top one to Georgia. When Georgia didn't say anything Skye looked at her, frowning.

"What?" Skye asked.

"What's up with you and Zak?"

"What do you mean?"

"I've been meaning to talk to you about it for ages. The things you do without him asking. The way you look at each other as if you're communicating in some way—a way without words."

"Well, we are." Skye laughed, not looking up from the grimoire she'd opened on her own lap. "He talks to me through our sire bond."

"Sire bond?"

"Yeah. You know, when Zak turned me into a vampire I was sired to him. Just like the other warriors. We all have this bond to him. Don't you? He turned you too."

"I have a blood bond with him. And a mind bond, when we mated. I haven't heard of a sire bond before. So he can what—talk to you telepathically?"

"Not talk, like we're doing now. But I just know when he needs me and he can sort of direct me where to go."

Georgia watched her sister's bent head for a minute, mulling over what she'd just told her. She'd never heard of the sire bond before, or that Zak could use it to control his vampires. She thought back over the last year, little things that had upset her about Skye when she'd first turned vamp, how when she'd mentioned to Zak that she missed the old Skye and then she'd suddenly started to wear her usual clothes again instead of the black warrior garb she'd adopted. Had Zak told her to? Had he taken away her free will?

That thought concerned her greatly and, rather than read the grimoire balanced on her knees, she absently stroked her belly and thought back over everything that had happened since Skye became a vampire. Realizing Skye was talking to her, Georgia dragged herself back to the conversation at hand.

"Sorry, what?"

"I said, should we call another meeting of the coven?"

"Not yet." Georgia shook her head. "I'd rather hold off until the boys can give us more information on who's behind the abductions. At least then we'd have some actual news to deliver."

Skye opened her mouth to speak, then froze. They both heard it. A scraping noise outside. Like a boot on gravel. Was someone out there? Pushing her senses out, Georgia tried to read the area but got nothing. Skye was looking at her, eyebrows raised, and she shook her head. She had a feeling someone was outside, but she couldn't say for sure and she couldn't pinpoint just who or what was out there. She didn't have to wait long to find out. The front door exploded and before she could so much as blink, icy cold fingers wrapped around her arm and began dragging her out of her chair.

5

"Hands off, asshole!" Skye flew at the black creature who had his claws wrapped around Georgia's arm and the two went down in a tangle of limbs, his hold on Georgia severed.

Struggling to her feet, Georgia threw magic at the beast, trying not to zap Skye in the process.

"Get down, Skye," she yelled. Skye dropped to the floor. A blast of magic shot across the room, slamming the demon in the chest and sending him sliding across the floor. To her horror, he rose to his feet, shook his massive head, drool flicking from his fangs and landing in globs on the floor. Shaking off her magical blast, he charged again. Skye tackled him around the waist, but this time he was ready. Raising her over his head he threw her through the front door, then turned his glowing red eyes on Georgia.

"Stay back!" Holding out her hands, Georgia fired more magic at him, and he staggered back a step but was gaining ground, fast. Shit.

As they circled each other, Georgia glanced around for a weapon, wishing she had her dagger within reach. She could feel her magic, swirling within her, full of angst. Then, as if a hundred witches were all speaking at once, in perfect unison, it came to her. A spell to banish the demon.

He growled, his lips peeling back. He was a massive demon dog-type beast, standing on two legs, over seven foot tall with arms and body like a man and a head like a dog, covered in black scales. There was a hint of sulfur in the air. Yes. It was definitely a demon in Carol's house, no matter what Zak thought. She knew she was right. The proof was right here, before her very eyes. And nose.

"Get away from her." Zak's voice was as cold as ice, the demon's big body blocking him from view. The demon swiveled, roaring again and launching at Zak.

"Daemon, relinquere hoc regno in perpetuum. Relinquere," Georgia shouted.

The demon vanished in midair, nothing remaining but the hint of sulfur burning her nose.

"Are you okay? Are you hurt?" Skye appeared by her side, concern on her face.

"I'm fine, what about you? Did he hurt you?"

"He threw me about a mile down the driveway! I don't think he wanted to hurt me so much as get me out of the way so he could get to you."

"What did you do?" Zak asked, striding toward her.

"A banishment spell."

"Will it hold him?" Skye asked.

Georgia shrugged. "I hope so."

"So...that's a demon." Georgia shuddered, gingerly lowering herself back into her armchair, her heart beating way too fast.

"Yes, he was a demon." Crossing to her, Zak cupped her face and looked into her eyes. "Take a breath. Slow that heart rate down, love. It's okay. You're safe now."

"Pft. I can protect myself, Zak, it just startled me, that's all. I've never seen a demon up close and personal before. And the smell!" She screwed up her nose.

"And the weird thing is, I still can't sense it. Even though I saw it here with my own eyes, I can't detect its energy signature at all."

"We're sitting targets." Closing her eyes, Georgia dragged in a deep calming breath. There was definitely a connection between the demons and disappearing witches, they just had to find out what. And how had the demon known where to find her? Did it follow them from Carol's house? Would more be coming?

"We can ward the house," Skye said, flipping open the grimoire on the coffee table and turning it so Georgia could see the pages. "There's a spell to keep demons out. And now that we know what we're dealing with, we'll ward the covens' houses too."

"Yes. Good." Georgia nodded, feeling light-headed.

"Babe?" Zak's voice, concerned, coming to her as if he were in a tunnel.

"I'm feeling a little...odd." She slumped back against the chair, out cold.

BLINKING, Georgia opened her eyes to a familiar sight. She was in bed, wrapped in Zak's arms.

"I'd really like it if you wouldn't do that again," he murmured, his voice rough.

"Sorry. Little adrenaline overload I think." Moving her hands to her stomach she felt for her baby and smiled softly when she felt a familiar kick against her palm. "We're okay." She was a little embarrassed that she'd passed out, knowing that Zak would seize on this and insist she stay home and do nothing for the sake of the baby, and while she loved that he worried, she also knew she could easily protect herself and would move heaven and earth to keep her baby safe.

"Did you ward the house?" She turned her head to look at him.

"Skye did. But you might want to check the spell since she's not technically a witch."

"Did you use my blood for the symbols?" He clasped her hand and lifted it so she could see the healing scratch across her palm. "We did."

"That should be enough to hold it then, but I'll check. What about the coven, has Skye contacted them?"

"They want to meet. Skye has the details."

She started to sit up, but Zak pulled her back down. "Nuh-uh. Not tonight. You can meet with them tomorrow."

"But the demon! I banished it back to its own dimension but that's not to say it can't come back, or that there aren't more to already here. I cannot lose another witch, Zak."

"I've sent the boys to keep watch over them tonight. For now, you need to rest."

A tingling sensation started where his fingers trailed up and down her bare back. She purred, arching into him. When she felt his lips at her nape, gently nipping, then kissing, she let out a groan. "I thought you said I should rest."

"You want me to stop?" He started to pull away and she turned in his arms, looping her arms around his neck and pulling his mouth to hers. "Don't you dare."

Easing from her embrace Zak made his way to the end of the bed where he knelt at her feet. Rising onto her elbows she watched him. Taking her right foot in his hand, he massaged her sole and instep with his thumbs. She flopped back onto the bed with a groan.

"Oh, that is so good." He hit all the right spots. The tired aching ones. She sighed in bliss when he switched feet. A zing of love shot through her heart. How she'd fought it when they'd first met, how furious she'd been that he'd seduced her in her dreams. And then he'd touched her for real and she'd melted into a puddle at his feet. She was his. He was hers. Fated. Mated.

Releasing her foot, Zak kissed his way up her body. Flames of lust licked through her at every stroke, every touch, every caress. Moving to her side he rolled her so she was facing him and wedged a thigh between hers. She rocked against it instinctively.

"Touch me," she whispered, aching for him. It had always been this way with Zak; they barely had to bother with foreplay, one touch and she was ready and primed for him, and her pregnancy had exacerbated her responses. Although they hadn't tried it, she was sure she could orgasm from his kiss alone.

Chuckling, he slid a hand between her thighs, stroking, teasing her clit while he captured a nipple between his lips and sucked. She jerked against him, weaving her hands into his hair and tugging his head closer to her. Her body was hypersensitive and she loved it. While she rocked and writhed against him, she reached down and stroked his erection, felt him pulse in her hand. His groan against her flesh made her crazy. She felt herself clench around him when he inserted one finger into her, muscles already tight, clamped around him. Releasing her nipple he dragged his mouth to her neck, sucking hard, grazing his teeth across her artery. She arched into him.

"Bite me," she whimpered.

"Not yet." He shook his head, his hair brushing against her face. "Look at me," he demanded. She opened her eyes, lost in the darkness of his. He lifted her leg over his hip and settled himself against her entrance, eyes drilling into hers as he pushed. Her eyes practically rolled into the back of her head as she stretched to accommodate him.

"No. Keep your eyes open," he growled, hips rocking, settling into a rhythm as old as time. She obeyed, drowning in his gaze as they rocked in sync, her body on fire for him. She felt herself winding tighter and tighter, climbing higher, her breathing coming faster, the sounds leaving her throat high and needy.

Then he dropped his head. She caught a glimpse of his fangs, felt the brief sting as they pierced the flesh of her neck, then nothing but bliss as he surged against her, hips pumping as he sucked her neck. Her orgasm hit hard and fast, shattering her into a thousand pieces.

6

"Thanks for coming, ladies." Georgia looked at the six women sitting around the kitchen table at her old farmhouse. Now that she lived with Zak in his big house ten minutes down the road, Georgia had decided to use her farmhouse as a meeting place for the Coven. And even though Zak had built her a wonderful workshop at his place, she still liked to come and use her workshop in the old stables here at the farm, although these days they mostly used it for spell casting.

"So what happened the other night? Why did you cancel the meet?" Raquel asked, taking a sip of coffee. Raquel was a fiery redhead who had made herself the designated spokesperson for the coven.

"I'm getting to that." Georgia stood at the head of the table, blew out a breath and dived right in. "You'll notice Carol isn't here tonight."

"Yeah, where is she? Did she quit?"

"No. She didn't quit. She's been abducted."

"What?" the women said in unison.

"What do you mean abducted? And by whom?" Raquel demanded, eyes narrowed on Georgia.

"We believe it's the work of demons," Georgia began, only to be cut off by Raquel again.

"We?"

"Myself, Skye, Zak and his warriors. There was a demon attack last night. On me. I don't have the answers as to why, or where they are, or if Carol is safe."

"Why didn't you tell us this sooner? How long have you known?" Leslie asked, a frown pulling her brows together.

"Carol was taken sometime yesterday. As far as I know, up until then, another two humans have been taken. I'm not sure what the connection is if there is one. But I can tell you there was a demon in Carol's house and now she's missing."

"Are you sure?" Lisa, the meekest of the coven, piped up.

"That demons are involved? Yes. Why? I don't know. We're still trying to sort through it all, but when a witch is targeted it's usually for her magic."

"Right. So you're not really sure, you're just guessing?" Raquel's voice was tinged with disdain.

"An educated guess."

"That demon's are kidnapping witches to what? Steal their magic?" This time it was Sheena who spoke, her voice incredulous.

"Yes," Georgia replied.

"So what do we do?"

"First of all, ward your houses to keep the demons out."

"How do we do that?"

"By drawing a symbol with your own blood and chanting a certain spell. We're going to ward this place now, so listen and watch carefully. Did you bring your grimoires? Take notes." Georgia turned to Skye. "Do you have our grimoire? Can you show them the symbol?"

"Sure." Reaching into the bag by her feet, Skye lifted out

the grimoire and opened it to the relevant page before placing it on the table. Lisa and Sheena leaned in close to look at the symbol on the page. An eye shape with a triangle overlaid.

"This symbol will prevent a demon from entering. You need to paint it onto every entry point. With your blood. Once painted, place your palm on it and recite these words. *Vade, daemonia. Animas vestras ad infernum remittitur.*"

The others watched as Georgia sliced her palm, dribbled the blood into a bowl, then painted the symbol on every door and window in the farmhouse and on the bricks above the fireplace with her fingertip. As she placed her hand over the symbol and repeated the spell the symbol glowed and then disappeared.

"Think you can do that?" Georgia asked when she'd finished warding the farmhouse.

"Yeah, got it," Sheena assured her.

"Once you've warded your home, you'll feel it, the bond to the ward, and you'll know if it's been broken or if it's becoming weak. In which case you need to re-do all of them."

"They can be broken?"

"Another witch can break them if she tries hard enough. Oh, keep in mind this ward is for demons only. It won't keep a vampire out. Or a were. Or an angel or any other paranormal. This one is specifically for demons."

The whole time Georgia was teaching the witches, she'd felt it. An undercurrent of...something. And it was coming from one of her witches. It was an angry energy and it niggled against her skin like a prickle in a sock.

"One more thing before we wrap it up for tonight." Georgia stopped them as they began gathering their belongings, getting ready to leave.

"Someone placed a hex on Mrs. Montanari's garden. Does anyone know anything about that?"

They all shook their heads, but Georgia couldn't help but notice Raquel wouldn't meet her eyes.

"While you might think hexing something or someone isn't a big deal, beware the use of dark magic."

"It wasn't us," Raquel protested, "have a little faith."

"Just keep your eyes and ears open, that's all I'm asking. Someone is dabbling and it could get dangerous."

After they'd left she stood on the front porch with Skye, watching the last tail lights disappear down the driveway.

"Ready to go?" Skye asked.

"Did you feel that?" Ignoring her question Georgia frowned, gazing into the darkness.

"What? Is something out there?" Straightening, Skye scanned the darkness.

"No. Did you feel the energy from the witches? Something is up. Something isn't right."

Blowing out a relieved sigh that a demon wasn't suddenly going to launch itself on them, Skye threw an arm around her sister's shoulders and squeezed.

"I'm sure they're just nervous. Shit's getting real. Come on, Zak will be waiting for us, we need to get moving."

"I DON'T LIKE THIS." Zak paced behind the park bench Georgia was currently perched on. In strategic places around the park, his warriors were stationed, waiting. After Georgia and Skye had shown the witches how to ward their homes, they'd met Zak and his warriors, ready to spring the trap they'd planned for the demons.

"I know you don't, babe. But we need to put a stop to these demons. I am not bringing our baby into this world with these assholes trying to hurt us." She was right and he knew it. The demons needed to be dealt with once and for all. And that meant capturing one and getting every piece of information out of it.

"Are you sure they're attracted to magic?" he asked.

"No, but it's worth a try." She shrugged. It was an educated guess. Why would a demon take a witch? Who knows? Again she didn't have all the answers. One that was still niggling at her was why humans had been taken too—were they a mistake? Maybe they had some psychic abilities that gave off a false reading? Or perhaps the psychic bond could be used as well. The question remained. Why? Why did the demons want the magic in the first place? And if it wasn't the magic they were after, why were they taking people? The only way to find the answer was to capture a demon.

"I'm only ten feet behind you. Do not get yourself killed." Zak dropped a kiss on her head and moved to conceal himself behind the wall of shrubs behind her. She'd figured the demons were attracted to magic, so she idly set the swings in the playground into motion, knowing even that small trick would be enough to alert them of her presence.

A half hour passed, the dark night pressing in around her. It was cold and she rubbed her arms, then wriggled. She needed to pee. Directly opposite her was a playground, and beyond that, public toilets. Gross, but it would have to do. Rising to her feet, she stretched, massaging her lower back.

"Going for a bathroom break," she muttered, knowing Zak would be able to hear her. She knew Skye was stationed at the toilet block, knew she would be safe, but Zak would be pissed she'd moved away from him. She grinned when she heard him growl.

She waddled toward the toilets. Using her magic she idly set the swings in motion again. That might hurry things along. She was level with the swings when the demon appeared, running across the park toward her at breakneck speed. Holding out her hands she sent a powerful wave of magic at him, stronger than what she'd used previously. The wave of magic sent the demon tumbling head over heels. That's when five vampire warriors leaped on him, pinning him to the ground.

As much as she wanted to stay and interrogate the demon, she still needed to pee. Badly. When she returned there was the heavy stench of sulfur in the air and black goo on the ground where the demon had been pinned.

"What happened?" She sighed. It was obvious though. They'd killed the demon. How could she get intel from him if he was dead?

"It took its own life." Frank stood looking down at the mess on the ground, shaking his head.

"What?" Georgia was incredulous.

"It's true." Kyan piped up. "Zak asked it who sent it and the demon bit its own arm and poof—or more precisely—splat. Self-destructed."

"Well. That was unexpected. And unfortunate." Georgia walked up to Zak and threaded her fingers with his. "But it does tell us one thing."

"Oh?" Zak asked

"That they are attracted to magic. It had no other way of knowing I was here. We made damn sure we weren't followed. And wherever they are based, it must be a reasonable distance from here. Let's assume it felt my first burst of magic when we arrived. That was what, about half an hour ago? And I just let out another little burst again, just as he arrived. On foot. So they must be about half an hour from here."

"He appeared at great speed," Aston commented. "And I would imagine he maintained that speed the entire journey. The goal would be to reach you as quickly as possible, so they could capture you. I can do some calculations and work out a radius for us to search."

"Won't more be coming?" Dainton moved to stand next to Skye and Georgia didn't miss the way her sister smiled at the warrior.

"Possibly," Zak agreed. "I would guess this fellow was their fastest. Backup could be coming. We need to get out of here. And no using magic." The last words he directed at Georgia, who frowned at him.

"Of course not. I'm not stupid. Our place and the farmhouse are warded. No demons will be getting in."

"We're not staying to fight them?" Cole asked, disappointment evident on his face. Zak shook his head.

"Not this time. This was an intel mission. We'll regroup, find their lair, and take them out there."

After taking Georgia home, with strict instructions to stay inside, Zak and the warriors left to search for the demons. Skye went with them after Georgia assured her she was going straight to bed. For the first time in ages, Georgia was on her own and she wasn't going to waste the opportunity. Letting herself out the front door, sending up a little prayer that Zak wouldn't be too mad that she'd disobeyed his instructions, she had one last thing she wanted to do before Jelly Bean arrived.

Driving to the cemetery, she grabbed the flowers she'd bought from the service station on the way and climbed down from the truck. The moon shone through the clouds, creating a dappled pattern on the ground. Approaching her parents' grave, she arranged the flowers, then stood looking at the headstone, tears filling her eyes.

"Mom. Dad. I want you to meet Jelly Bean. My baby. I really wish you could be here, Mom, for her birth. I never really imagined having kids and now that it's here, I'm kinda terrified." Wiping away a stray tear, she drew a shuddering breath. "I don't know what I'm doing. I don't know how to be a mom. I need you here to teach me." A sob tore from her throat, then another, until she fell to her knees, wave after wave of grief washing through her, over her, until she was drowning in it.

"Sweetheart, stop those tears," her mother's voice whispered in her ear, and she sucked in a breath.

"Mom?" Swiveling around she gasped at the apparition before her.

"It's me. Your little Jelly Bean brought me. She's a special one for sure."

"She is." Georgia's smile was watery. "It's so good to see you."

"And you, but I can't stay. I want you to know I'm always with you. Even though you can't see or hear me, your father and I are watching over you and Skye. We might not be here in person, but we are here in spirit. Never forget."

"I won't forget, Mom," Georgia promised, breathing in the scent of her mother's perfume.

"Skye is going to need you soon." Her voice started to fade, her physical body started to shimmer. She was leaving.

"Why? What's wrong?"

"Her heart will be broken."

"What? By Dainton? I'll kill him!" Georgia swore.

Her mother smiled, reaching out and touching her cheek. "So protective of your little sister. She will be fine. What happens is the natural course. But do not let her shut herself away from you. Help her heal."

"I will." Closing her eyes, Georgia felt the kiss her mother pressed to her forehead. When she opened her eyes she was gone. "Bye, Mom." The wind whispering through the trees was the only reply.

She knelt on the ground in front of the headstone for a while, embracing the sense of peace that had replaced the grief.

"Thank you, Jelly Bean." She smiled when Jelly Bean moved against her hand. "Right. Now I need to get up." She moaned, struggling to her feet. It took three tries, but eventually, she managed to get off her knees. Walking back to her truck she smiled, her fears and doubts about the impending birth and motherhood eased.

"WHAT? I don't know what you're talking about, Georgia. I swear!" Dainton held his hands up, not quite touching Georgia who had him pinned against the wall.

"If you hurt my sister I'm going to ram your gonads so far up your ass you'll be able to taste them. Do I make myself clear?" she snarled, her face an inch from his, her forearm pressing hard against his throat.

"I won't hurt her. I swear!"

"Georgia!" Skye came running, word of their argument spreading through the house like wildfire. "What's going on? What did he do?"

"It's what he's going to do that's the problem." Georgia glared, not taking her eyes from him.

"I'm not going to do anything, I swear to God. I like Skye. A lot. I'm not going to mess that up."

"You do?" Skye squeaked, shifting her weight from foot to foot as she stood behind her sister.

"I do."

"I have it on good authority that you are going to mess it up." Georgia's anger practically sizzled on her skin.

"Who?" Skye and Dainton spoke at once.

"Mom. I spoke with Mom."

"What?" Skye's voice rose several octaves. "How did you speak to Mom? When?"

"I went to the cemetery this evening after you all went

46

demon hunting. Jelly Bean brought her to me. She told me you were going to be heartbroken." Georgia had turned her head to speak with Skye, but when Dainton sucked in a breath she swiveled back to him.

"Yeah. You, dickwad," she snapped.

"No. Georgia, let him go. He hasn't done anything." Skye grabbed her arm and tried to pry her away. "And if he does, well, then you can have at him."

"Fine!" Georgia's eyes blazed as she drilled Dainton with her angry stare. "But I'm watching you, buddy. One wrong move."

"Got it," Dainton muttered, shuffling sideways and out of the door.

"What was that?" Frank asked from the doorway.

"Nothing for you to worry about." Georgia pushed past him, heading back into the house.

"Wait up!" Skye called, running after her. "Jeez, for a pregnant woman you sure can move fast. What else did Mom say?"

"Nothing. Just that she and Dad are watching over us."

"I wish I'd been there." Skye's voice held a hint of sadness and Georgia stopped, spun, and embraced her sister.

"If I'd known it was going to happen, I'd have taken you with me," she reassured her. She'd gone to have a private word, to share her worry with the one person who would understand—her mom. She'd never expected to get a reply!

8

S itting at the end of the sofa, Zak pulled her feet into his lap and began to massage.

"Oooooh, that's so good." She closed her eyes and lost herself in the bliss of his touch.

"What happened here today?" he asked, thumb pressing into the arch of her foot. "I felt some high emotion from multiple people."

"You're not going to like it," Georgia mumbled, not opening her eyes.

He stopped rubbing. "What?"

"I went to the cemetery. To visit Mom and Dad's grave."

"Georgia." He sighed, shaking his head. "What if the demons had found you there, defenseless?"

"I'm pregnant, not helpless, and certainly not defenseless." She jerked her feet away, but he grabbed her ankles and settled them back on his lap. "You know I can deal with the demons. I've got more power than any of you, yet you keep treating me as if I'm defenseless, wanting to keep me at home where it's *safe*."

"Did something happen at the cemetery?" He deftly brought her attention back to the topic at hand.

"I saw Mom. Jelly Bean brought her to me."

"What? Jelly Bean what? Explain."

"I was a bit emotional. I wanted Mom. You know, I'm about to give birth and I wanted my mom. And she appeared. She told me Jelly Bean sent her, that she and Dad are always watching over me and Skye. And that Skye was going to experience heartbreak and I needed to look after her."

"Okay. Wow. So the spikes I felt from Skye and Dainton—I assume that was you, getting up in Dainton's business?" He grinned, resuming the foot rub.

"Yes. It's embarrassing how well you know me," she admitted.

"What happened?"

"He said he really likes Skye and has no intention of hurting her." Georgia sighed.

"He's a good man. He wouldn't toy with Skye's emotions. He already knows he'd have me to deal with. And now you. And quite frankly I think you're the more scary option."

"Pft. Of course. He already has visions of his balls lodged in his throat, so yes, he took heed."

"But you have to let them work it out for themselves, babe. You don't like anyone, family or not, interfering in our relationship. As much as you want to protect Skye from any hurt, you've got to let her lead her own life, make her own decisions. And mistakes."

"You're going to make an awesome parent." And if she was honest, it made her jealous. She hated the thought of Skye's feelings being hurt and wanted to protect her at all costs, but Zak was right. She couldn't wrap her in cotton wool. Just be there to help put the pieces back together when whatever was going to happen, happened. A thought drifted across her mind and she frowned. "Why haven't I seen it?"

"Seen what?"

"Skye's heartbreak. Mom warned me, not to stop it from happening, but to be there for her after, to help her through it. Why haven't I seen it myself, a vision? Something?"

"You've said before that you've never had a vision of Skye, that when you try and see her future you get nothing."

"Maybe it's because we're related? I didn't see Mom and Dad's car accident coming either. Perhaps it doesn't work on blood relations?"

"Could be." Zak pressed a little harder, distracting her from her thoughts. He knew she spiraled into an angry depressive state when she thought of her parents' death and how she hadn't been able to prevent it. But everything changed when the Hunter arrived and revealed the truth. He was behind their deaths; it was all orchestrated by him and whoever was pulling his strings.

"You're distracting me. On purpose." Pulling her legs away, she swung around until she was sitting up, suddenly angry at Zak.

"I'm trying to keep you calm."

"I don't need to be kept calm. Stop treating me like a fragile flower." Her temper was ramping up and Jelly Bean kicked against her ribs. Hard. Okay, so maybe Zak had a point and she needed to stay calm. Sucking in a deep breath, she focused on blowing out the anger.

"You're all wound up. Come on, let's go take a bath."

Oh, he was sneaky. He knew all her favorite things. She especially loved baths with Zak.

Hand in hand they climbed the stairs. While Zak got the water running in their big tub, she snapped her fingers and the candles lit with a flame. Grinning at Zak in the candlelight, she hooked the hem of her T-shirt in her fingers and tugged it over her head. Her maternity bra was the next to go and she delighted in Zak's intake of breath, the way his pupils dilated looking at her. As her body had grown and changed he'd never made her feel less desirable—if anything he made her feel the exact opposite. As sexy as all hell.

She started to shimmy out of her jeans when he knelt at her feet and helped her out of them. Holding onto his shoulders for balance she lifted one foot, then the other, while he freed her feet from the tangle of denim. Clad in nothing but her less-than-sexy panties, she looked down at him kneeling before her. Holding her gaze, he hooked his thumbs into the waistband of her underwear and whisked them down and off.

Much to her disappointment, he rose to his feet, lips curled in a smirk. With an exaggerated sigh she placed her hand in the one he held out to her and allowed him to help her into the tub. Settling in she closed her eyes in bliss as the warm water lapped around her, soothing her aching body. Then she remembered, and her eyes snapped open, just in time to catch Zak stripping. Her favorite part. Climbing into the tub with her, he settled at the opposite end and rubbed her calves, his hooded eyes never leaving her face.

She loved that he took such great care of her, smothering though it could be at times.

IT HAD BEEN three days since the trap at the park that had resulted in one dead demon and Georgia's midnight trip to the cemetery. Three days of being confined to the house, Zak refusing to let her leave, even to travel to the farmhouse, despite it being warded. Aston had calculated a circumference of where he thought the demon could have traveled from and the warriors had diligently been searching, but so far, nothing.

Flicking through the magazine on nursery ideas Zak had

bought her, Georgia nibbled on a muffin and tried to distract herself from being housebound. She knew Zak was keeping her confined because he worried, and she went along with it for she knew there wasn't much she could do to help at the moment. Once the warriors tracked down the demons' lair, then she'd be all in, but for now, she let Zak think he was having his way and she was doing as she was told. Her phone buzzed, and she glanced down at the screen, a smile tilting her lips when she saw who was calling. A friendly chat with one of her witches was the perfect solution to her current boredom.

"Jess. What's up?"

"Help! We need help. I think it's a demon!" Jess was shouting, and the sound of glass breaking could be heard in the background.

"It broke the wards?" Georgia slid off the barstool and rushed to the front door, keys in hand.

"Missed—" Jess was cut off. Georgia could hear the phone as it hit the ground, the sounds of a struggle, grunting and screaming, then a loud crunch and the line went dead.

"Shit. Shit. Shit." Running to her truck, she had the key in the ignition when Skye appeared in the passenger seat.

"What's happening?" she asked.

"A demon. At Meghan and Jess's place."

"I'll call Zak." Skye pulled out her phone and dialed as Georgia fishtailed down the driveway.

"Fuck. We're too far away. They'd only be able to hold a demon off for a minute. Two tops. It's going to take us twenty to get there!" Georgia cursed, speeding down the highway, not caring if she copped a speeding ticket.

"Zak and the guys are closer. Just take a breath and concentrate on your driving, please. The last thing we need is for you to have an accident."

Skye was right. She was driving recklessly. If she lost

control and the truck flipped she risked not only herself and Skye but Jelly Bean too. Her foot eased off the accelerator. Zak and his warriors were in town. Closer. Skye had given them Meghan and Jess's address. They'd get there in time—they had to.

She scraped five minutes off her arrival time. Screeching to a halt, she threw open the door and rushed across the front lawn to the house sisters Meghan and Jess occupied. The big old house had been in their family for generations and the two sisters shared the place now that their parents had retired and moved to the coast.

The closer she got to the house, the more pungent the smell. Sulfur. And she could feel it. Demon. The front door stood open, much like Carol's house, only this time it wasn't empty. Zak and his warriors were inside.

"Where are they?" She puffed, stumbling to a halt in the living room. The place was a shambles, worse than Carol's place. Blood spattered one wall.

"Not here." Zak's face was grim.

"It took both of them?"

"I think there was more than one demon. Although I still can't feel their signature, can you?"

"Yes. And the smell is stronger. So they knew two witches lived here. One demon per witch, to subdue them."

"They put up a hell of a fight." Zak nodded at the blood on the wall.

Turning away Georgia leaned one hand against the wall behind her, head bowed. She couldn't believe this was happening. The wards should have kept them safe.

"How did they get in?" she asked without looking up.

"Basement. There's an old hatch out the back, external access. Hidden by shrubs, but you can clearly see where the shrubbery has been pulled back and the padlock ripped off."

"They either forgot to ward that entrance or they didn't

know about it." Georgia sighed. Once a demon gained entry it didn't matter how many wards you had on the other entrance points, they were all void. "Damn it!" She punched the wall, pain radiating up her arm from the impact.

"Hey!" Zak grabbed her wrist, stopping her from punching again. "This isn't your fault."

"They're my witches! It's my responsibility to keep them safe. I should have come by and checked all the wards."

He pulled her into his arms. No words could ease the burden she felt. She'd failed them. Three of her witches were in the hands of the demons—the only thing she knew for sure was that they were still alive. Which also meant they were most likely suffering. Whatever the demons wanted them for, it wouldn't be pleasant.

Pulling herself from Zak's embrace, she turned, looking for Skye.

"Call the Coven. We need to meet."

Skye looked to Zak and when he nodded she pulled out her phone. "On it." Georgia got the look that passed between the two and frowned again.

"You and I are going to have a conversation real soon." She stabbed a finger into Zak's chest. He looked at her in surprise.

"Hey! What's that for?"

"The way you're controlling my sister. I can't believe it took me this long to notice it, but now that I have, I'm not happy about it. Not happy at all."

"Babe—" he began, but she cut him off.

"No. It will have to wait, but until then, stop ordering her around. We'll discuss it once my witches are found and the demons are dealt with."

"But—"

"I mean it, Zak. I want you to break the sire bond with her. Think on that."

She whirled away, stomping back to her truck. Angry at Zak, angry at herself, furious at the demons, and worried that the dark angel she'd seen in her vision hadn't put in an appearance yet. Who was he and what was he waiting for?

———

"WHAT CAN I GET YOU?" Eddie asked. Georgia sat on her usual barstool, a feeling of nostalgia washing over her. Eddie ran the pub across the road from the antique store Georgia and Skye owned. She'd bought *Behind the Times* with the inheritance money from her parents' death – Skye had managed the store, purchasing old pieces of furniture from garage sales and auctions and Georgia had stripped them down and brought them back to life. Back then, life had been simple. No vampires. No witches. No demons.

"Well, circumstances say I can't drink alcohol but can I *please* just smell it? It's been a tough few days."

Eddie barked out a laugh. "Okay. That's right up there with some of the strangest requests I've received. What would you like to smell? Whiskey? Scotch?"

"Beer. I'll pay for it. I just can't drink it."

"Coming right up." Eddie turned away to get her drink and she leaned her elbows on the counter, fiddling with a coaster. A glass full of amber liquid appeared in front of her and she leaned over, inhaling deeply.

"Oh, that is so good." She closed her eyes, imagining the taste of the beer on her tongue.

"When's baby due?" Eddie asked.

"Another month."

"Do you know what you're having? I know my niece found out her baby's sex really early on in her pregnancy, what with all the newfangled technology they have available these days."

Georgia shook her head. "Technically no, but I think it's a girl."

"You're not drinking that, are you?" Skye appeared at her shoulder, nodding at the tall glass of beer in front of her.

"No. Just smelling it." Georgia barked out a laugh. "I really want to though."

"I got hold of the coven. They'll be here soon. Did you need me to get anything?" Sliding onto the bar stool next to Georgia, Skye gave her a wan smile.

"No. I have everything I need."

"What can I get you, Skye?" Eddie appeared, smiling.

"Oh, I'll just drink hers when she's done sniffing it." Skye nodded her head at Georgia's drink.

"Man, it sucks not being able to drink," Georgia grumbled, leaning forward to take another whiff. "I miss it."

"Profits have been down since you got knocked up." Eddie laughed and Georgia poked her tongue out at him.

"Never thought you'd see the day, eh, Eddie?" Skye teased.

"What, this wildcat settling down and having a baby? You got that right."

"Awww, you two, don't make me smack your heads together." Georgia threatened through a chuckle. "Eddie, I'm hungry."

"God, again?" Skye looked at her aghast. "You don't stop eating!"

"I'm eating for two," Georgia pointed out.

"What'll it be, love?" Eddie asked, whipping out a notebook to take her order.

"Burger and fries. Double fries. Extra pickles."

"Anything for you, Skye?" he asked.

"No, I'm good, thanks, Eddie. I value my arteries."

"You know what I miss?" Georgia sighed.

"Besides beer?"

"Yeah. Besides beer. I miss Rhys. How many times have I

sat on this barstool and he's swaggered in and parked his ass next to me?"

Skye slung her arm around her sister's shoulders and squeezed. "I know you miss him. We all do. I'm sure it's just pack stuff though. He kinda got thrown in the deep end when the Alpha died."

Again Georgia's heart ached over the death of the Alpha and his wife and their unborn child. Her own baby kicked against her ribs and she chuckled, grabbing Skye's hand and pressing it against her abdomen.

"Someone wants to say hello," she explained.

"Well hello there, Jelly Bean," Skye spoke to Georgia's stomach in a cooing baby voice.

"She's hardly a Jelly Bean anymore." Georgia laughed. "More like a watermelon."

"She?" Skye cocked a brow. "Are you having a girl?"

"Don't know." Georgia shrugged. "It's just a feeling. I hear her talking to me sometimes and the voice is female, but it might not even be Jelly Bean I'm hearing. It could be the witches' magic."

"What are you hearing exactly?" Skye frowned.

"Just encouraging words really. Like it's okay. Be strong. That type of thing. Not conversations or anything like that."

"That's incredible." Skye breathed. Georgia shrugged again. Incredible and amazing had become her new normal. She'd gone from a reluctant human psychic to a vampire with psychic abilities to a witch–vampire hybrid who had the power of hundreds of witches coursing through her veins. And on top of all that, she was pregnant by an angel-vampire hybrid. Nothing in her life was normal anymore, so hearing her unborn baby talk to her? Didn't faze her at all.

"Here you go, love." Eddie appeared with her burger and fries and she dove in, demolishing the whole lot within minutes.

"Christ, haven't you eaten today?" Eddie laughed.

"I'm always hungry." Georgia grinned, wiping her face with a napkin. "I can seriously eat anything and not put on any weight *and* still feel hungry."

"Can I have the beer now?" Skye cut in.

"Sure. Eddie, I'll have a soda, please." The girls sat in silence, sipping their drinks until Georgia's back began to ache. She glanced at the time on her phone.

"The others should be here any minute." It was time for the coven to meet.

9

"What do you mean, Meghan and Jess have been taken?" They'd been sitting around a dining table at the pub. Georgia had felt it was too risky to meet at the farmhouse, but now Raquel rose to her feet, cheeks flushed.

"They missed an entry point when they warded the house. A demon got in." There was no easy way to put it.

"And?" Raquel demanded. Georgia frowned. What did she mean "and"?

"What are you doing about it?" Raquel elaborated.

"We're searching for them of course," Georgia explained. She understood Raquel's anger, hell she was angry herself, but they needed to work together on this, to stay strong and present a united front. "But in the meantime, I need you to *not* use your magic. Somehow they're tracking us through magic."

"Bullshit. I don't believe you." Raquel remained standing, anger radiating from her. "You want us to sit on our hands and do nothing. To hide. If we band together we can defeat these so-called demons. You're being too cautious; we need to be on the offensive."

There was muttering among the women and Georgia realized at least some of them agreed with Raquel.

"Look, we don't know how many demons there are. The one that attacked me was big and powerful and fast. We have a spell to banish demons—Skye will send it to your phones—but until we know exactly what we're dealing with, please, please, just do as I ask. We need to plan, we need to know what we're dealing with before we go rushing in blindly. If our witches are still alive, and I sense that they are, we could risk their lives if we act rashly."

"You're risking their lives by sitting here doing nothing," Raquel shot back. "You say you have a spell to banish demons. Let's do it then, banish them."

"Raquel, you know nothing of demons. Zak does. He says they're not working alone, that someone is giving them orders. It's not as simple as banishing all the demons. We're working on a plan."

"What plan?"

"We haven't nutted out all the details yet, but rest assured, we are working on it."

There was silence around the table. Raquel was still standing, shifting her weight from foot to foot as she looked around the table. Then her eyes met Georgia's.

"I don't believe this is the right course of action for our coven. I think you're blindsided not only by your pregnancy but also your relationship with a vampire. It pains me to say this, but I hereby disavow myself from your coven." By the smirk on her lips, Georgia got the impression it didn't pain her at all and perhaps she'd been planning some sort of coup all along. "Ladies, if any of you would care to join me, I would be delighted to have you. I am proposing a new coven. Led by me."

Jenna and Leslie both stood and Georgia's heart sank. She loved all the members of her coven, even Raquel. To have them leave her hurt. And frustrated her because she knew they didn't believe the severity of the situation or the danger they could be placing themselves in.

"Raquel. Please reconsider." Georgia stood as well, hands rubbing her belly. Raquel looked at her with pity.

"You're being overly cautious because of your baby, and I can understand that, Georgia, but if you weren't pregnant would you be telling the coven not to use magic? To hide? I don't think so. You'd be all in, guns blazing. Maybe you need to take maternity leave and leave the witchcraft to us."

Her words stung and Georgia felt a flare of anger. In the past, she would have pinned the woman to the wall with an arm across her throat, but maybe she was right. Maybe pregnancy had changed her, for she let her walk away, taking half of her coven with her. She felt the break as they passed the threshold of the door, like the snapping of a rubber band against her soul. Thunder rumbled even though the skies were clear. The sound of magic separating.

But with it came clarity. What she couldn't see before, she could see clearly now. Raquel was the one who'd hexed Mrs. Montanari's garden. The question was, why? It was dark magic. Why was she messing with that when everything Georgia had taught her was to use light? She'd have to pin down Raquel another time and have it out with her. Right now she had other things to worry about.

"That probably drew some attention," she told Skye and sent up a prayer that by the time the demons came to investigate everyone would be safe in their homes.

"We're still with you, Georgia." Lisa and Sheena smiled tentatively and Georgia tried to wipe the worry from her face.

"Thank you. I'm sorry for all of this. I swear your safety is all I'm thinking about."

Lisa nodded. "Your plan makes sense. We need to know

what we're dealing with first, not go rushing in blindly. Know your enemy."

"This isn't what you signed up for when you joined the coven." Georgia ran a weary hand over her face before sinking back onto her chair.

"Oh come on," Sheena chuckled, "you laid it on the line from day one. You and your baby are the next generation of witches. A stronger breed. A prophecy that's been thousands of years in the making. Of course, someone's going to try and stop you. Us. If it came as a surprise to anyone, then all I can say is they're probably not the right fit for this coven anyway."

Sheena had a point. Georgia had been upfront and honest from the get-go. They'd known about her aunt's betrayal that had resulted in the death of her entire coven. They all understood what was at stake. But it still stung that she hadn't been able to keep her coven together. It had only been a few short months and here she was with a mutiny on her hands.

Everyone's phones gave a beep and Skye glanced up. "That's just me. Sent you the demon banishing spell. And yes"—she addressed Georgia—"I sent it to Raquel and her new coven." Skye used air quotes for the new coven. "Not that they deserve it."

"Skye," Georgia chided, "I wish them well. I get the sense Raquel was never really happy with us. She's probably been looking for an excuse to break away for a while. You don't set up your own coven on a whim. She's been planning this."

"That makes it all the worse." Skye frowned. "Zero loyalty. Karma will sort her out."

Ignoring her, Georgia addressed the two witches seated at the table. All that was left of her coven.

"Ladies, write the spell in your grimoires and practice it. Pronunciation is important— if you get a word wrong, it won't work, and a demon won't stand around waiting for you to get it right."

"Can you take us through it?" Lisa asked.

They spent the next half an hour going through the spell. Thankfully the pub was busy and it was doubtful anyone overheard them. Skye excused herself at one point and returned with fries for everyone. Once full, Georgia sat back in her chair, feeling melancholy. So much had changed. She'd gone from having a coven of eight down to a coven of three in a matter of days. But that wasn't what bothered her the most. What bothered her was the abducted witches. Why did the demons want them?

"Let's walk," Skye suggested after Lisa and Sheena had said their goodbyes.

"Good idea." Stepping back, Skye gave her room to maneuver out of her chair, following close behind as Georgia headed outside.

"Everything okay?" Skye asked.

"Yeah, I'm good, I just can't stay in one position too long. Bubs is squashing all my organs."

"Oh good. Well, not good about your squashed organs but good that you're okay. Speaking of bubs, Lisa and Sheena are talking about holding a baby shower for you."

"A baby shower?" Georgia snorted. She wasn't a baby shower type of girl. "Can you nip that one in the bud for me?"

Skye laughed. "I'll see what I can do. But in all serious-ness, it's not a bad idea. I know you haven't got everything you need for baby's arrival."

"I've got a cot," Georgia protested.

"That you made yourself. At some point, you're going to have to go shopping and buy the baby clothes, blankets, nappies."

Georgia stopped and looked at Skye. "Nice try, but I'm

not stupid. I know all of you have been sneaking baby things into the house. Zak included. You think I'm wandering around oblivious to what's going on under my own roof?"

"Damn it. We wanted it to be a surprise."

"I know you did. Which is why I didn't say anything. Anyway…I have bought baby stuff. I can be as sneaky as you guys. It's in the workshop at the farm."

"I have a sneaky suspicion Jelly Bean is going to be the most spoiled baby of all time." Skye patted Georgia's belly and the baby kicked in response.

"She likes the idea of that." Georgia laughed. They'd slowly walked away from the bar, but now, up ahead in the darkness, something shone under a streetlight, catching her attention. Was that a demon?

"Shh." Grabbing Skye's hand, she pulled her in close against the building and pointed. Yes, darting along the street, keeping to the shadows, was a demon, the light reflecting off its scales each time it moved beneath a lamp post.

"Let's follow," Skye whispered, "I can take him." It was true, after Marius had left Skye for dead, Zak had saved her by turning her into a vampire. Skye had embraced her new vampire life, including training alongside the others to become a warrior. Coupled with Georgia's magical abilities, they were well equipped to deal with a lone demon.

"Let's see what he's up to." Georgia darted ahead, keeping to the shadows like the demon had. She ducked into a doorway when it stopped, looked back towards them, then turned into an alley. Once it was out of sight the girls continued to follow it.

"Do we follow it into the alley? It could be a trap," Skye whispered.

"Just a few feet. Is this one a dead end?"

"I don't think so."

Creeping forward they stepped into the darkness of the alley, crouching low to give their eyes time to adjust. Up ahead a big Dumpster blocked half of the alley, providing cover. They scrambled up to it, pressing close against its side as if to blend with it. It was silent in the alley and Georgia feared the demon had passed straight through when the sound of voices reached their ears. Frowning, Georgia strained to make out what they were saying, but it was no good, the voices were muffled. Standing up, she peered over the top of the Dumpster and there, at the far end of the alley, she spotted the demon. Talking to a Nephilim. A startled gasp escaped and she quickly hunched back behind the Dumpster, Skye frowning at her.

The voices stopped. Shit. Did they hear her? Holding her breath she slowly released it when the two began speaking again.

"You know it's imperative we find the witches. We need them for the purge, the city cannot be cleansed without it." The voice belonged to the Nephilim, his angelic tones clearly identifiable to Georgia.

"Yes," the demon agreed.

"Then what are you waiting for? Go. Get it done."

They could hear the sound of the demon's footsteps as he hurried from the far end of the alley. Then silence. Where was the Nephilim? Was he still there? Georgia had recognized him for what he was immediately. Even though he didn't have wings, he had a certain aura and her psychic senses had picked up his signature. As a human-angel hybrid, a Nephilim had no magic, although they possessed super-human strength and intelligence, not to mention they were fearless, which made them an opponent to be wary of.

"You can come out now. The demon has gone." His angelic voice sounded from the other side of the Dumpster and she pressed a hand to her chest in shock. He moved in total silence. Blowing out a breath, she pressed a hand to Skye's shoulder, urging her to stay hidden as she eased to her feet and looked over the Dumpster.

"I almost didn't sense you," the Nephilim told her.

"If I'd been quieter you wouldn't have known I was here at all," Georgia replied.

"True. You're surprised I'm a Nephilim?" he asked.

"More likely confused as to why a Nephilim is hanging out with a demon."

"You overheard?" He arched a brow but didn't appear surprised. And why would he, he'd known she was there.

"Some," Georgia admitted.

"Then you know we're on a mission to rid the city of witches. Considering some of your coven have been taken, I'm sure that's no surprise to you."

"How do you know about me and my coven?"

"Research." The Nephilim smiled, his good looks mesmerizing. At least to humans they were. To Georgia, his appearance had no impact. He couldn't use charm to lure her in. He clued in pretty fast when she didn't react the way he expected her to.

"I'm going to have to ask you to come with me, Ms. Pearce." His smile twisted into something evil and a shiver ran down her spine.

"I'm going to have to decline on that," Georgia responded, squaring her shoulders, sensing an attack was imminent. She was right. Suddenly an object was flying through the air at her. She blocked it with her magic and it clinked to the ground at her feet. A throwing star. Interesting choice of weapon. Before he could dispatch another, she flicked a wave of magic at him that sent him flying backward, tripping over his own feet and skidding on his back in the dank alleyway.

"You'll pay for that," he growled.

"Doubtful." Georgia kept hitting him with bolts of magic,

but he was managing to shield himself somehow. She needed to end this skirmish now.

"Skye," she grunted, "call Zak."

Skye stood, revealing herself and the Nephilim looked at her in surprise. As Georgia had expected, he'd had no idea she was there.

"No need, between the two of us we can take him." Skye rounded the Dumpster, cracking her knuckles, ready to unleash hell on the Nephilim.

The Nephilim threw a handful of throwing stars, his movements lighting fast. Skye was faster, dodging them all and closing in fast when the unthinkable happened. One found its target in her shoulder. She swore, then staggered, trying to stay on her feet. She cast a look at Georgia, confusion on her face.

"Get back here," Georgia yelled. "*Now!*"

Skye pulled the star out of her shoulder, dripping blood. Then her eyes rolled into the back of her head. The Nephilim caught her as she fell.

"Rookie error, vamp." The Nephilim sneered, licking the side of Skye's face and making Georgia shudder.

"Let her go," Georgia demanded.

"Tell you what, I'll exchange her for you," he offered.

"I don't believe you would. You'd keep us both."

"Smart witch. She's the key to controlling you. I'll be keeping her." Dragging Skye backward to the end of the alley, he cast one last look at Georgia, a grin of triumph on his face.

"Be seeing you, witch." Then he disappeared, taking Skye with him.

10

"Shit, shit, shit." Georgia kicked the side of the Dumpster in frustration, cursing when pain radiated up her leg.

"Georgia? Skye?" Hearing Zak call, she made her way out of the alley, spotting him further down the street.

"I'm here," she replied, watching as he swiveled then appeared in front of her.

"Skye summoned me. Is she with you? And just what are you doing here exactly? You should be at home resting." Grabbing hold of her arm, Zak began walking her back toward the bar. Pulling her arm free from his grip, she stopped, hands on hips, and glowered.

"First of all, I'm fine, thanks for asking. Second, I was meeting with my coven. I needed to teach them the demon banishing spell. And finally, a Nephilim has taken Skye."

"A Nephilim?" Surprise colored his voice. "You'd better start at the beginning."

"We saw a demon and followed it into this alley." She indicated the alley behind her. "We hid and heard the demon talking with someone else. His energy pattern told me it was a Nephilim. Then the demon left, but the Nephilim knew we were there...well, he knew I was there. So we had a bit of a skirmish and it would have been fine, but then Skye decided she could take him. Instead, he turned the tables and took her. He was using throwing stars. I think they must've been coated with some sort of poison since the one in Skye's shoulder knocked her out. I couldn't use my magic against him when he was using her as a shield."

"Shit. So what? You think the demons are working with the Nephilim? And you're sure it was a Nephilim?"

"Yes, I'm sure it was a Nephilim. And yes, it appears they're working together. I couldn't hear everything, but the Nephilim was telling the demon he needed to get the witches to purge the city."

"Purge the city. Interesting."

"Have you heard of that before?" she asked.

"I have a feeling I've heard it somewhere, but I can't remember where." Zak ran his fingers through his hair. Pulling out his cell phone, he dialed, all the while keeping his eyes trained on Georgia.

"He's behind the witches being abducted. He told me so. Now that I know his energy signature I can probably trace him. Find him, Skye, and the witches."

Wrapping his arm around her shoulders, he pulled her in tight, raising his cell phone to his ear. "Frank. Skye has been abducted. Gather up the boys, we've work to do." He gave Frank instructions on where to find them, then rubbed his hand up and down Georgia's back.

"She'll be fine," he soothed.

"Probably. It's just—she always seems to get taken when it's me people are after."

"Skye can take care of herself, she's a trained warrior. And maybe this will turn out to be a good thing. Not only will we get Skye back, but she'll lead us to the other witches."

"Maybe."

Within minutes two SUVs pulled up. The warriors had arrived. Helping her into one of the waiting cars Zak briefly spoke with Frank before joining her.

"Okay. Can you trace them? Which way?"

Closing her eyes she focused on the Nephilim's energy pattern, guiding the warriors through the city to an abandoned warehouse on the other side of town.

"Wait in the car," Zak told her but she shook her head.

"No way. You're going to need my help."

"Sweetheart, we've got this."

"Yeah, that's what Skye said and look how that turned out. You're forgetting I've got a shit ton of powerful magic that can protect us all."

"Argh." He rolled his eyes. "Why are you always so damn stubborn?"

"You wouldn't have me any other way and you know it." Lowering herself out of the car, she quietly closed the door and clasped Zak's hand.

"Aston, Dainton, and Cole take the far side of the warehouse. Frank, Kyan, you're with me." The warriors moved away at vampire speed, so fast Georgia couldn't track their movements. Frank and Kyan went ahead, while Zak threaded his fingers with hers and matched his pace to her pregnant swagger as she picked her way across the unkempt parking lot to the side of the warehouse. It was dark: no light shone out of the warehouse, no streetlights to light the way.

Zak's phone vibrated in his pocket and he pulled it out. "Yeah?" He listened for a moment and then hung up.

"That was Aston. They're in position. They can see Skye inside, with three demons guarding her. They're going to create a distraction on that side of the warehouse, give us time to get in and get Skye out."

"The other witches?"

"No sign of them. But they could be in there somewhere. We'll find them."

Hunkering down against the side of the warehouse, they waited for the signal. They didn't have to wait long. A loud boom rang out from the opposite side of the warehouse. Footsteps could be heard running.

"Now," Zak commanded. Frank kicked the door in and they piled inside, Zak keeping Georgia tucked behind him. "Go untie Skye. We've got this."

Reaching her sister who was tied to a chair in the middle of the warehouse, Georgia tore the tape from off her mouth before crouching behind her to free her bound wrists.

"It's a trap," Skye gasped pulling frantically at the chains that bound her hands.

"What?" As the words left Georgia's lips, a dozen Nephilim swarmed the warehouse, outnumbering them.

"Georgia!" Zak roared, appearing by her side.

"I'm okay," she assured him, throwing out waves of magic, blasting the Nephilim, sending them skidding along the floor to crash into the wall with a thud.

"Dainton! Behind you!" Her scream hurt her throat. Dainton looked over his shoulder, started to turn to grab the Nephilim behind him when the sword in its hands cleaved through his neck. Dainton toppled, his head rolling inches from where his body lay. Dead.

"Nooooooo!" Skye screamed, running toward him. "No. No. No. You can't be dead. You can't be!" Skidding to her knees by his side Skye frantically rolled him to his back, tugging his head back to his body as if trying to reattach it. Behind her the Nephilim raised his sword, ready to take down his next victim.

"Oh no, you don't." Frank launched, knocking the sword from the Nephilim's grip and taking him down. Georgia stood frozen in disbelief, eyes unseeing as Skye frantically tried to heal Dainton.

Suddenly Zak was behind her, sweeping her off her feet with an arm beneath her knees and another beneath her shoulders. He whizzed her out of the warehouse, heading toward the cars.

"Get in and drive. Don't stop, not for anyone. Don't argue, just do it!" He deposited her beside the vehicle and disappeared before she could even open her mouth. Fumbling with the door handle, she opened the door and climbed in, flinching when the passenger door flew open.

"It's just me. Go. Drive." Aston slid in, slamming the door. Twisting the key in the ignition Georgia peeled out, flicking on the headlights as she went.

"Skye?" she asked, heart beating frantically. She couldn't believe Dainton was dead. No healing, no magic could bring any creature back from decapitation. A tear trickled down her cheek, unheeded. Unless Zak's ring could do it, it had the power to restore life to immortals. Then she remembered. He had to die at the hand of her dagger for the ring to work. Another wave of despair hit her. There was no getting out of this, Dainton was truly dead.

"Zak will bring her home," Aston replied, his voice gruff.

Georgia kept driving, but images of Dainton kept creeping into her vision and with the tears wetting her cheeks, driving was almost impossible.

"You're shaking," Aston pointed out. "Pull over. I'll drive." Without a word she did as instructed, switching places with him. They were both silent for the rest of the journey. When they pulled up in the driveway, Zak was waiting.

"Dainton?" she asked, rushing to him.

He wrapped her in his arms and held tight. "He's dead."

It was customary to burn a dead vampire's body as soon as possible after death, to release their spirit. Zak prepared Dainton's body alone, strapping his corpse to a wooden stretcher and wrapping it tightly in fabric, like a shroud. There were only two ways to kill a vampire. Pierce their heart—or rip it out of their chest as Georgia had done to Veronica—or a beheading.

While Zak got Dainton ready, the warriors prepared the pyre. They'd chosen a remote spot on the banks of the river several miles west of Redmeadows. They wouldn't be disturbed here. Frank walked the perimeter of the pyre, whispering a prayer in a language Georgia had never heard before, while the warriors stacked wood upon wood. Then Zak appeared, carrying the stretcher with Dainton strapped to it in his arms. The warriors rushed forward; two on each side they carried Dainton to the pyre and placed him on it, heaping more wood on top.

Skye stood wordlessly to one side, unaware of the customs playing out in front of her, unable to participate, frozen with grief, tears tracking silently down her face. Her arms hung limply by her sides, still covered in Dainton's blood. Georgia crossed to her, the packed earth uneven beneath her feet, and threaded her fingers with her sisters, uncaring of the blood. Skye's blue eyes were bruised and empty.

"I..." Skye tried to speak, but no words came out.

"You loved him." Georgia nodded. She knew that to be true. No matter their relationship was new, Skye had loved Dainton.

"I loved him," Skye whispered in response, her composure crumbling. She cried out loud, wrapping her arms around Georgia, burying her face in her neck. The two women stood while the vampires finished the pyre. Then Zak's voice broke through Skye's sobbing.

"We're ready."

Straightening, Skye wiped her arm across her eyes and sniffed. Keeping hold of her hand, Georgia clasped Zak's with the other.

"Ashes to ashes, brother." He nodded, and Frank lit the pyre. The wood went up with a whoosh, the flames dancing high, consuming Dainton's body.

"Dainton was a warrior. Our brother." Zak's voice rang out, steely authority hiding the pain that was surely tearing him apart inside. "He was brave, fearless. He died an honorable death, protecting those he loved. Go now in peace, Dainton. May your spirit soar free, unencumbered by earthly bonds."

"Go in peace," the warriors repeated.

"Go in peace," Skye and Georgia whispered in perfect unison. They stood in silence until eventually, Georgia cleared her throat.

"Can I? Can I say something?" she asked, turning her head to look at Zak, the firelight throwing shadows across his face. He inclined his head, squeezing her hand still tightly clasped in his.

"I've lost too many people in my life. People who I thought would be by my side forever have been taken from me. The worst part of loving someone is the day you lose them. Go in peace, Dainton, you'll be missed."

Silence followed, the only sound the crackle of the fire as they stood staring into the flames, hypnotized, thinking of their own mortality, watching as Dainton's body was consumed by flames.

One thought went around and around in Georgia's head. This is what her mom had meant. Dainton didn't intentionally hurt Skye. He died.

She stood in Zak's arms as the flames danced brightly in the night sky. Even Jelly Bean was still. She listened as each of the warriors said goodbye to their fallen friend, their voices gruff with emotion. Her own heart ached at the loss of one of their own.

Hours passed. Zak left, only to return seconds later with a chair for Georgia. He stood behind her, hands on her shoulders until the flames had died down and a breeze blew, sweeping up the ashes, twirling them in the sky like a corkscrew before scattering them into the river. Georgia stirred, tearing her eyes from the pyre to her sister, who was sitting in the dirt, a forlorn mess.

"Skye." Her voice barely a whisper, she struggled to her feet, crossing to her sister and resting her hand on Skye's shoulder. "Time to get cleaned up."

Skye glanced down at herself, at the dried blood staining her shirt and hands. Nodding, she struggled to her feet, her eyes empty. Georgia wrapped her fingers around Skye's, wincing at the icy coldness of her skin, and led her to the vehicles, the warriors falling into a line behind them. She could only imagine the grief she was going through. If she lost Zak, hell, she'd throw herself on the funeral pyre to be with him.

***

"THEY WERE EXPECTING WITCHES," Skye explained later that evening, her voice hoarse from her tears, her face pale. They'd all retired to their rooms to catch some sleep before the hunt continued.

"How do you know?" Zak asked. He was subdued. They all were. But they still had a threat hanging over them, and now the stakes were higher. They had a death to avenge.

"They told me so. They were very cocky. Strutting around saying how Georgia would bring her coven of witches to rescue me and they'd basically be serving themselves up on a silver platter."

"We at least had some element of surprise then," Frank muttered, sitting at the large conference table where they'd congregated in the front room.

"It's all about the magic. I heard them saying they want to harvest the witches from the city, and purge them for their powers. I don't know why, but I think I know how they're finding the witches."

"How?" Georgia's head snapped up.

"They have these weird electronic devices. Devices that track magic. They knew you were coming because they were tracking your magic," Skye told her.

"Interesting. A device that tracks magic," Aston commented, swiveling to his keyboard and punching in God only knows what.

The baby kicked and Georgia rubbed her hand over her belly. It wouldn't be long until she met her precious baby in person. She couldn't wait to hold her in her arms. This mess had to be sorted before then.

"Sweetheart, you get some rest," Zak said. "You're exhausted. We'll keep going, see what we can find out. I'm curious as to how and why all the Nephilim that have descended on Redmeadows are working with the demons." He slipped a hand beneath her nape and tilted her face to his.

"I think I will. I'm beat." She sighed, closing her eyes, feeling the brush of his lips against hers and a peaceful calm settle over her. Everything would be okay. It had to be.

11

"Hey, sleepy head." Zak's voice roused her from a deep sleep. Groaning, Georgia rolled to her back, an arm flung over her eyes.

"What time is it?" she mumbled, trying to free her mind from the cobwebs of sleep.

"Seven."

"A.M.? Why wake me so early?" She sat up, untangling herself from the covers.

"P.M. You've slept for about eighteen hours." He chuckled, holding out a hand to haul her to her feet.

"What? That's ridiculous. Are you pissing in my ear?" Narrowing her eyes in suspicion she cast a glance at the window. The heavy drapes blocked everything, and she couldn't tell if it was day or night. But something told her she'd been asleep a fair while, like her overfull bladder and growling stomach.

"I think I'm going to wet myself." Clenching her knees together, she began to shuffle toward the bathroom when Zak scooped her up and rushed her to the toilet, depositing her gently on her feet.

"Can't have that. I'll get Frank started on breakfast. Or should I say dinner? Any requests?" Turned out Frank was quite the cook, a skill that had gone unnoticed when it was just vampires in the house who didn't eat food.

"Pancakes. Lots and lots of pancakes. With lemon and sugar. And maple syrup. And strawberries."

Closing the door, she could hear Zak's laughter as he walked away. Once she'd dealt with her bladder she took a quick shower, slipped into one of the few items of clothing that still fit—a black and white striped T-shirt dress—and headed downstairs. Her stomach growled again as she approached the kitchen, the scent of pancakes in the air.

"Here you go." Frank slid a stack of pancakes in front of her.

Georgia shoved so much in her mouth she could barely chew, then closed her eyes as the flavors exploded on her tongue. A steaming cup of decaffeinated coffee appeared at her elbow.

"Thanks," she muttered, mouth still full.

"No problem. So, now that you're awake, we have news." Cole slid onto the stool next to her, face serious.

"What's that?" Finishing her mouthful of pancake, she pulled the coffee toward her and took a sip. At least it tasted like the real deal, even if it was missing the caffeine kick.

"Aston found a lead. A rogue vampire. Apparently, he might know something that can help us."

"Where?"

"He's meeting Zak at a bar in town tonight, in a couple of hours."

"And before you ask, no, you're not coming." Zak strolled into the kitchen, Aston close behind him.

"Do we have to have this same argument over and over again?" Georgia sighed dramatically, eyes rolling. "You'll say I can't come, I say I'm coming anyway and guess what? I'll be there. You know it, I know it, let's not waste time. Sweetheart." The last word dripped sarcasm.

"Are you sassing me?" Zak's eyebrow arched as he filled a cup from a blood bag and put it in the microwave to heat.

"You have to ask?" she shot back, winking. He threw back his head and laughed.

"Okay, hit me with it. What's your argument for coming with me tonight and not staying here where it's safe?"

"You already know I have kickass magic skills. I can look after myself, and Jelly Bean. But you keep forgetting—*you* have the power to destroy the demons. You have your own brand of magic that can take them out just like that." She snapped her fingers to demonstrate.

He shook his head in denial. "My magic is dangerous. I can't control it. If I lose control I could destroy the entire planet."

"I saw what you did in Eden Hills. You wiped out the horde of demons with your magic, you didn't destroy anything or anyone else. Just the demons. You've got more control than what you give yourself credit for. You were given those powers for a reason, Zak. Just like the ring was created to restore life to immortals and the dagger to bring death to immortals. Just like little Jelly Bean and I are part of this ancient prophecy. Jelly Bean is the baby from your vision, she has to be…the ring and dagger will be united and a child born of prophecy shall walk the earth. It's all happening, whether you like it or not. I'd much rather be fighting with you, by your side, than staying here without you. Together we are stronger. Plus, I can do this." With a slight movement of her hand, she used her magic to slap everyone's head in unison.

"Hey!" They protested, rubbing the back of their heads where she'd zapped them.

"I only have to amp that up just a little, and boom, you're

incapacitated. All of you. Even you." The last words were for Zak alone.

The room was silent as everyone took in her words. She let them absorb them before continuing.

"And you know I would never, ever risk Jelly Bean. I'd get myself out of there, even if it meant leaving you—and the others—behind. I'd go."

"Promise?"

"Promise."

Shaking his head, he stood across the kitchen bench from her and, leaning forward, pressed a hard kiss to her mouth.

"Deal."

THE BAR WAS A REAL DIVE. A handful of motorbikes were parked out the front, the neon sign above the door was half broken, and the place stank of stale booze and urine.

"Delightful," Georgia muttered, keeping hold of Zak's hand as they crossed to the bar. A bald barman with a scar etched deep in his cheek took his sweet time coming to serve them.

"What'll it be?" His tone indicated he didn't particularly care.

"I'm looking for Aren. I was told he'd be here tonight."

The barman nodded his head to the left and they turned, seeing a skinny, unkempt man sitting in a tattered booth. Thanking the barman, Zak led the way, gesturing for Georgia to slide into the booth before taking his seat next to her.

"Aren?" he asked.

"Yup. You must be Zak. Who's this?" He nodded toward Georgia, his greasy hair barely moving.

"She's none of your concern. I'm told you had some information for me."

"For a price." He wiped at his nose and his eyes darted from side to side.

"Cash or blood?" Zak asked.

"I get a choice?" He seemed surprised. Zak shrugged. He had plenty of both. If Aren had the information they needed he'd be rewarded appropriately. "From the vein?" Aren's eyes darted to Georgia's neck and Zak stiffened beside her.

"Cash it is." Zak's voice was icy cold and his fingers clenched on the table top.

"Fine. Two thousand."

"If the information is useful, it's a deal. If you're just spouting bullshit I'll take you outside and beat the living shit out of you. Clear?"

"Crystal." Clearly, Aren had done this before; he wasn't bothered by Zak's threat.

"What do you know about the demons and Nephilim?"

"Here's what I heard." Aren leaned forward, elbows on the table. "The demons have partnered with the Nephilim to serve an angel called Ronan. He's the boss. He's footing the bill."

"Footing the bill for what? What is it that this Ronan wants?"

"He wants the witches. All of the witches. Each witch has a bounty, the demons cash in when they capture one."

"What does he want the witches for?"

"Their magic. I heard he wants to take their magic and transfer it to the Nephilim."

Georgia looked at Zak, her eyes filled with concern. "How are they finding them?" she asked Aren.

"They've got these gadgets, little black box things that track magic."

"That's what Skye said," Georgia muttered, "back at the

warehouse. That they were tracking me because I was using my magic to find them."

"You're a witch? An important one I'd imagine if you're here with this guy." Aren's interest picked up and she sat back against the cracked vinyl of the booth, putting as much distance between herself and Aren as she could.

"Don't even think it," Zak growled.

Aren laughed, leaning back, hands up. "Take it easy, man, I'm not a bounty hunter. Anyway, I think what I've just told you proves my worth."

"Do you know where we can find this angel, Ronan?"

"Nope."

Zak looked at Georgia, who shrugged. Aren had already given them a lot. It would be too much to hope to have all the pieces fit nicely together.

"Here. Two for your info, another two to keep your mouth shut. We weren't here. She isn't a witch." Zak tossed the money onto the table and Aren quickly snatched it up.

"Wasn't here," he muttered. Jumping to his feet, stuffing the money into his pocket, he left. Minutes later they heard the roar of a motorbike.

12

Georgia looked at the black device in Cole's hand. It didn't seem that remarkable, but according to Aren, it had some outstanding technology within its plastic casing.

"Where did you find it?" she asked. They stood in the backyard where Georgia had been practicing her knife-throwing skills.

"In the warehouse where Skye was taken. I was pretty sure one of them doofuses would have dropped one. It was buried under some debris, but yup, I found it."

"It couldn't have been easy," Georgia muttered, "going back there."

Cole shrugged. "Had to be done. Was the logical place to look. And if it means avenging Dainton's death, I'll do anything, go anywhere."

She nodded at his words. It was true; all of them were different now, all had wounds that only time would heal.

"Do we know how it works?" Georgia asked.

"This looks like the on button, so if I slide that over, it should work." He moved the button and sure enough a light on the device began to flash.

"I guess it's picking up on me?" Georgia asked, holding out her hand for the device. Cole passed it to her and the flashing light turned red, then a beeping noise started.

"What's it doing?" She frowned over the noise. Running toward her, Zak snatched it from her hand and tossed it. It exploded midair.

"What the hell? It was a bomb?" Feeling the baby kick, she rubbed her stomach, talking softly. "It's okay, Jelly Bean, Mummy's all right."

Zak turned to her, cupping her chin. "You okay?"

"I'm fine. But why would it do that? Are they rigged to explode?"

"Doubtful. I'm wondering if you have too much magic. Maybe it overloaded? But now we've lost our one piece of evidence. I'll see what Aston can retrieve from it."

They hurried over to where the device was now scattered across the ground, Zak and Cole gathering up the pieces. They all turned when they heard a car in the driveway.

"That sounds like..." Zak began but Georgia cut him off, "Rhys's car!"

She took off around the side of the house. Sure enough, Rhys's 4WD sat in the driveway. He grinned when he saw her.

"Well, you've put on a few pounds." He teased, stepping forward and wrapping her in a bear hug.

"Where the hell have you been? And why haven't you returned any of my calls or messages?" To her utter horror, emotion overwhelmed her and she burst into tears. She'd missed him so much and had been so worried about him, now it was overwhelming to have his handsome, goofy face in front of her.

"What did you do?" Zak growled, assessing her wet face and stabbing Rhys with his steely gaze.

"Nothing, nothing, I swear." Rhys peered at her, frowning. "I've got no idea why she's crying. Hormones?"

"Yes, it's bloody hormones, you moron!" Georgia punched him in the shoulder and he staggered back a step. "Still pack a mean punch, I see." He laughed, then sobered. "But seriously, we need to talk."

"Not until you tell me where you've been and why you've been avoiding me."

"I haven't been avoiding you and I'll tell you everything. But right now we don't have time. Right now a group of witches—I do believe they are yours—are trying to take down a bunch of demons."

"What? Are they insane?" Cole burst out.

"Quite possibly." Georgia pinched the bridge of her nose. "I bet it's Raquel. My coven fractured. She's taken some of my witches and started her own coven. Is this witch a redhead?"

"She is." Rhys nodded.

"Bloody hell. Where are they?"

"An old warehouse on the far side of Redmeadows."

"Do you think it's the same place they held Skye?" Cole asked.

"Possibly," Georgia replied. "You'd better lead the way," she told Rhys.

"I'll take the warriors with me." Zak gestured his warriors to gather around. "Rhys, I'm trusting you with her. Keep her safe." He nodded toward Georgia.

"Always," Rhys assured him. "Where's Skye?"

"She's dealing with some stuff," Georgia told him. "I'll fill you in on the drive." The truth was Skye refused to come out of her room. When they'd returned from Dainton's funeral, Georgia had to shower her, dry her and dress her in night-clothes before putting her to bed. It had been as if Skye was awake but comatose.

Zak disappeared with the warriors and Georgia climbed into the passenger seat of Rhys's truck.

Once the truck was in motion and they were heading into town, Georgia looked at Rhys. "Are you okay? Are you good? Is the pack okay?"

Laughing, Rhys reached over and patted her leg with one hand. "We're all fine. The pack is great. We're settling into our new life, I'm learning the ropes of the construction business that Hayden owned. He was doing good things. I want to continue that."

"Will you leave the force?" She placed a hand over his, knowing just how much he loved his job on the Redmeadows Police Force.

"I think I'll have to. There's only so much of me to go around, and now that I'm living at Hayden's old place, well, it's a long commute every day." The Alpha had property at least an hour's drive out of Redmeadows, a great big house where his pack could stay when they needed to, and plenty of space for them to run. He'd also owned a construction company, but now that he was dead, it all belonged to Rhys.

"So spill—why haven't you been returning my calls?" Georgia crossed her arms, waiting.

"I've been tracking this angel, Ronan."

That name again. "We know of him." Georgia nodded. "You know where he is?"

"I do. I stumbled across him accidentally a while back, realized he's involved in something shady so I went undercover and observed his operations. Pretty sure if we work together we can take him down."

"Agreed. But you could have told me about this sooner," Georgia scolded.

"Oh yeah? And have you racing in, guns blazing, distracting me and blowing my cover? Yeah, no." Rhys had a point. That's exactly what she'd do. Sighing, she looked out the window.

"Enough about me. What about you? You sure there's only one baby in there? You're huge!"

"Pretty sure it's just the one, but the ultrasound won't work on her. She's blocking somehow."

"She?"

"I have a feeling the baby is a girl." Georgia grinned, resting her hands on top of her baby bump. "We've been doing great, up until this whole demon and Nephilim thing. For a while, things were relatively peaceful."

"Too good to last."

"Yes. But yes, things have been good. I've been getting my coven together, Skye has done a brilliant job in getting the shop re-opened, and business is booming."

"So what's with Skye? Why isn't she here?" he asked.

"Dainton was killed."

"What? Holy shit! How?"

Georgia told him the story, wiping tears away as she recounted the night at the warehouse. The same warehouse they were possibly traveling to right this minute.

"That's full-on. I've been gone too long. I didn't know Skye and Dainton were an item." Rhys shook his head in disbelief.

"It was new. I don't think they were officially dating, but I know she had real feelings for him."

"That really sucks."

"I know. And I didn't see it coming. Again! What's the point of being psychic if you can't protect the ones you love?"

"It's about balance, Georgia." He glanced at her before turning his attention back to the road. "All magic has to have a balance. So for you, you can see people's future's, just not your own or—your family's? Or those you love?"

"So you're saying it's the price I have to pay? For having this ability?"

"In a way. Light balances dark. Good balances evil. You get my drift? There has to be a balance. Nature demands it."

"That does make sense. So what is the price I'm going to have to pay to have a miracle baby?"

"I think you've already paid it," Rhys told her, shrugging.

She looked at him, confused. "What do you mean?"

"Well, you're no longer a vampire. That was the price. You gave up immortality to become a witch. As a witch, you can conceive."

"But...I didn't give up being a vampire. I'm a hybrid," she protested.

"Are you? When was the last time you drank blood?"

"Ummm. About ten months ago."

"And don't you think, since you're growing another being inside you, that your appetite would be increased, that you'd need *more* blood, not less?"

"I've been craving food," she whispered, amazed at his insight. How hadn't she figured this out for herself before now?

"And walking around in daylight—that didn't clue you in?"

"Well, I used a daylight protection spell. On me and the others."

"Maybe you should break the spell and see what happens. Would that convince you?"

"I've never heard of a vampire reverting back." Although both her aunt and the Hunter had touched on that very topic at one point or another.

"You didn't really revert back," Rhys explained, "you evolved. So your body became human—up to a certain point —then witchcraft took over."

"But witches are human."

"Are they?" Rhys started to slow the truck and Georgia realized they were indeed headed for the warehouse where Skye had been taken. Shit.

"Ummm, Rhys? This place? Last time we were here there were a ton of Nephilim and demons. We couldn't beat them then; it's doubtful we can this time. Also…this is where Dainton died."

"Good to know. Let's focus on getting the witches out of there then."

Turning into the parking lot, Rhys killed the engine. Before he opened his door he turned to Georgia.

"Zak will kill me if anything happens to you. Please, *please*, stay here. Pick off any strays that stumble out, but otherwise keep clear."

"Rhys…" Georgia whined, frustrated at being kept out of the action, especially when she knew it wasn't necessary. She could protect herself and Jelly Bean or she wouldn't have climbed into his truck in the first place.

"Promise me." Rhys met her eyes, his own a whirlwind of emotion. "I couldn't bear for anything to happen to you, Georgia. Please."

Guilt over the death of Hayden and Angela washed over her again and she nodded her head. She owed him. Through helping her she'd gotten them killed. Rhys would be angry at her for eternity if she got herself or the baby hurt. Not that she'd risk Jelly Bean. Never gonna happen.

"Okay."

"Stay in the truck." Rhys slid out and softly closed the door behind him. The wait was interminable. Georgia leaned forward and eyed the warehouse. Thinking of her sister, she pulled out her phone. No answer, but then she hadn't really expected one. Skye had shut herself in her room, not wanting to talk with anyone. The call went through to voice mail.

89

"Hey, Skye, it's me. I know you said you wanted to be alone, but I'm just checking on you. Call me if you need me. I love you."

Hanging up, she listened to the shouting and sounds of fighting coming from inside the dilapidated building. Through the side door of the warehouse, a body came tumbling out, a demon barreling after it.

"I've got this." Georgia slid out of the car. *"Daemon, relinquere hoc regno in perpetuum. Relinquere,"* she whispered. The demon vanished.

Raquel pulled herself to her feet, wobbly, blood running down her face. Shit, shit, shit. Georgia watched as the redhead took a step toward her, looking as if a stiff wind could knock her down. Shaking her head in resignation, Georgia hurried as fast as she could toward Raquel. She had to get the other woman out of here.

"Raquel. It's me, Georgia. Come this way, quick," she whispered, grasping Raquel's wrist and tugging her toward Rhys's truck.

"Georgia?" Raquel squeaked, squinting in the darkness.

"Quickly. *Come on!*" Tugging harder, Georgia began to drag Raquel, who appeared confused and disorientated. Given the gash on her forehead, Georgia wasn't surprised. At least she wasn't dead. Yet. They were almost to the car when Georgia felt it, a change in the air, a heaviness. Then she heard it. An ominous laugh behind her. Glancing over her shoulder, she saw the dark angel from her vision. Ronan.

13

Swiveling, Georgia pushed Raquel behind her.

"Knew you wouldn't be far away." Ronan smiled. He really was very attractive, but then Georgia surmised all angels were, fallen or not. His blue eyes sparkled and his blonde hair was impeccably styled. She wondered where angels went to get their hair cut when he broke into her thoughts.

"Your witches are mine." He gloated, taking a step toward her. Holding out her hands Georgia sent a pulse of magic at him, frowning when it didn't so much as bounce off of Ronan, it almost caressed him it had so little impact. What the hell?

"Not the effect you were looking for, little witch?" Ronan laughed, moving closer. She knew angels had different levels of magic, obviously Ronan had some sort of protection spell going on. Georgia shuffled back, bumping into Raquel.

"Get into the car," she told the other woman. Keeping her eyes on Ronan, she could hear the shuffle and scrape of Raquel's feet then the sound of the car door opening.

"Tell you what, little witch, since you amuse me so, I have a proposition for you."

"Oh?"

"You give me the baby and I'll let everyone go. I'll even let your vampire friends live."

Sucking in a breath, Georgia wrapped her arms around her stomach and turned sideways, trying to keep her swollen belly away from Ronan.

"Over my dead body," she spat.

"If you insist." Ronan leaped at her and she blasted another wave of magic at him, and again it bounced off. Damn it! While she wasn't entirely powerless without magic, it certainly helped. Especially since she couldn't move as fast as she once did. She just needed to get her dagger out of Rhys's car where it sat in the footwell. She cursed herself for getting out of the car without it.

Turning, she ran, skidding around the back of the car. Damn, she wished she had her boots on and her dagger in her hand, that would slow the bastard down. She felt him grab for her, felt the brush of air where his fingers just missed her neck. Close. He was so damn close. Shooting down the side of the car, she grabbed the hood and pulled herself around the front of the vehicle, feet sliding in the gravel.

She couldn't keep this up for long, running around and around Rhys's car. She sent out a thought to Zak, knowing he was acutely attuned to her, that he'd be here in a microsecond. Her distraction cost her. Ronan caught her wrist, his grip as cold as ice, and she let out a startled yelp.

Suddenly Zak appeared, his fist jabbing into Ronan's throat. It was the distraction Georgia needed. Ronan's grip loosened enough for her to pull free. Running for the warehouse, she spotted Rhys running toward her and could have cried with relief.

"Are you hurt?" he puffed, seeing the way she was cradling her wrist against her chest.

"I'm fine. Help Zak."

Standing in the middle of the parking lot, unsure which way to go, Georgia watched as Zak and Rhys fought with Ronan. A tangle of limbs and flying fists, the fight moved away from the car, back toward the warehouse. They hit the outside wall with a loud crash, the aged building groaning loudly in protest.

"Jenna! Leslie!" Georgia screamed, looking for the other witches. She didn't have time to stand around and watch them fight, she had to get her witches out.

"Here. I've got them, get in the car, we need to get out of here." Cole was dragging Jenna and Leslie with him. Rushing to Rhys's car, she opened the back door for Cole to push the witches in, then slid behind the wheel, adjusting the seat to her shorter legs. Thank God Rhys had left the keys in the ignition. As soon as Cole climbed in next to her she peeled out of the parking lot, wheels spraying gravel.

Zak would get Rhys and the others out of there. It was up to her and Cole to get the witches to safety.

"You should have listened to me," Georgia muttered, glaring at Raquel in the rear view mirror.

"I'm sorry." Raquel whimpered, "We thought we were strong. We were nothing. Our magic was as powerful as an insect bite."

"How badly hurt are they?" Georgia asked Cole.

"They're okay. Bit banged up, but they'll live. Where should we take them? I doubt their homes are safe."

"We warded them!" Raquel protested.

"Yes, but now you've given the demons and the Nephilim a taste of your magical essence. They can follow you home and simply wait you out. As soon as you step foot outside, bang, they've got you. Or the Nephilim can simply break in and take you. The wards don't work against them," Georgia explained. "We'll take them to our place where we can keep an eye on them. It might give Skye something to do, a distraction."

Cole's phone buzzed and he pulled it out. Georgia listened in as he told Zak they had the witches and were taking them home. At least their house had a concealment spell, everyone should be safe there. As soon as she'd killed the engine after pulling into the driveway the driver's side door flew open and Zak was pulling her into his arms.

"I'm fine. We're both fine," Georgia protested.

"He had hold of you." Zak's words were deep, cold, full of rage.

"And thanks to you he released me." Placing her palm against his cheek, she looked into his eyes, willing him to calm down. Slowly his breaths deepened, the flush on his cheeks subsided, and he closed his eyes, blowing out a breath.

"Let's go inside, shall we, folks? Where it's protected?" Cole prompted, ushering them into the old mansion and closing the front door firmly behind them.

"Is everyone okay?" Georgia asked, glancing around to make sure all the warriors were accounted for. Rhys was leaning against a wall in the lounge room and waved his fingers in a salute at her.

"Yup, we're all good." Kyan cracked his knuckles. "That was a tough one though. Those demons didn't want to go down. And the Nephilim! Are those dudes indestructible or what? Cannot believe Ronan managed to slip away, sneaky bastard."

"Ronan got away? Damn it." Georgia cursed. They needed to find out who this dark angel really was and stop him from stealing the witches' magic. He was strong and had hidden talents of his own, if they were going to win this, they had to find out everything they could about him.

"Time to do some research, Aston, and find out what sort of weapons we need to take them down, once and for all," Zak said. Aston nodded and left for the front room where his computer was set up.

"Cole, can you take Raquel, Jenna, and Leslie upstairs, settle them into a guest room. Let Skye know they're here, that we need her help." Georgia nodded toward the wan-looking witches who stood huddled together. Without a word, Cole motioned to the staircase and the women duti-fully headed upstairs.

"Go get cleaned up," Zak told the others and they filed out of the room. Rhys sank into an armchair, watching as Zak helped Georgia onto the sofa, lifting her legs onto the cush-ions so she could recline. She still cradled her wrist to her chest and Rhys nodded at it.

"You hurt your wrist?" he asked.

"What? You're hurt?" Zak was kneeling by her side in an instant, prying her fingers from her wrist.

"It's where Ronan had a hold of me. It burns," Georgia admitted, lifting her hand away. She showed them the inside of her wrist where a dark mark the shape of Ronan's fingers marred her skin.

"Is that a bruise?" Rhys peered over the back of the sofa for a closer look.

"Looks like it. Get her a cold pack from the freezer."

"You could just heal me?" Georgia reminded him.

"And risk Jelly Bean? Your rules, remember. No trans-porting, no healing, no using magic on you."

"You're right. Something happened out there tonight that puzzles me." Georgia leaned back against the cushions, wrig-gling to get comfortable. Impossible at eight months preg-nant, but she tried.

"My magic didn't affect him. It was like he had a force field and it bounced off of him. We need to find out what he is, exactly, and what his powers are. And then stop him."

"We just need to figure out how."

Georgia rubbed at her wrist, frowning at the mark. Something told her it wasn't a bruise. Something told her it was something a lot worse.

14

Twelve hours later the gray bruise on her wrist was now almost black. Tugging down the sleeve of her blouse, she covered the mark, hiding it from Zak. He'd only worry, and worrying didn't solve anything. They needed answers.

Maneuvering her bulk downstairs, she followed the sound of voices to the front room. There she found Aston, Cole, and Frank sitting at the conference table.

"What's happening, guys?" she said from the doorway.

"Oh hey, you're up. Hungry?" Frank pushed back his chair and stood.

"Starving, as always." Georgia shrugged, giving Frank a smile as he rushed past her telling her breakfast was on its way. It was a godsend he had such fantastic culinary skills. Easing herself into the closest chair, she looked at Cole. "Whatcha doing?"

"Trying to work out Ronan's game plan. What does he want, what will he gain from gathering all this magic? And how do we stop him?"

"How's that going?"

"Slowly," Cole admitted.

"Here you go." A steaming cup of coffee appeared at her elbow and she took a sip.

"Thanks, Frank." The first month of her pregnancy had been the worst for caffeine cravings. Thankfully her body was now used to doing without, but still, a cup of real coffee would hit the spot right about now, rather than the decaffeinated brew Frank presented her with.

"We found some symbols in the warehouse, but can't work out what they mean." Aston projected his laptop monitor onto the big screen. A photo of five symbols that were scratched into the brick wall of the warehouse appeared.

"With the spacing, it kinda looks like some sort of writing. Like Egyptian hieroglyphics," Georgia commented.

"Agreed. But we can't find a reference anywhere. We've already documented pretty much every symbol in your grimoires. It's not witchcraft."

"Demon language? Do they even have a language?" she suggested.

"It seems we don't know as much about demons as we thought we did. We never thought they could be organized and work together—we were proven wrong in Eden Hills, and again here. It seems demons can be trained, as long as they have a leader, someone to direct them."

"Do you think this is connected to the attack in Eden Hills?" Georgia asked, wanting to know their opinions before delivering her piece of news.

"I don't see how. That was almost two years ago. Why wait? Why now?"

"I have a theory," Georgia said. "One that I put together from a vision I had recently."

"Oh?" Aston and Cole sat back, faces eager.

"In my vision, I saw Zak's place in Eden Hills being

attacked by demons. And I saw Zak wipe them out. But I also saw Ronan at the scene."

"He was there?" Aston's surprise was evident in his voice.

"In my vision, he was there. You may not have noticed him at the time. You were distracted."

"With what?"

"By the ring activating…" She trailed off, waiting for them to put the pieces together.

"Wait. You think Ronan was there for the ring?"

"Think about it," she prompted. "Me and Jelly Bean are the prophecy. The ones who start a new generation of powerful witches. Good witches. Witches that could stop all sorts of evil. If you had some less-than-pure plans to carry out, you wouldn't want these witches to be created, would you? You'd want it stopped. And if you knew about the prophecy, you'd try and stop it at the very beginning. He didn't know where the dagger was, it had been hidden for eons, but the ring had always been in Zak's possession. And the only way to get it from Zak? To kill him. The ring can only be removed upon his death. So by killing Zak he'd not only destroy the ring, but it would stop Jelly Bean from being conceived."

"And if you knew about the prophecy, you'd have to be an immortal too." Cole breathed, nodding his head.

"I would say so. Or at least have access to ancient knowledge. We need to talk to Zak, see if he can remember who knew about the ring and dagger. They've been kept secret for eons. It's possible it was someone who was there, at the beginning. He might even know what the symbols mean." She glanced around. "Where is he anyway?"

"Checking on Skye and the women," Frank said, placing a plate piled high with bacon, eggs, baby spinach and fried tomatoes in front of her. A side plate held two pieces of toast dripping with butter. She drooled.

"Thank you," she muttered before shoving in a mouthful of food, keeping her attention on her plate while she thought about the symbols.

"There has to be a connection between Ronan and Zak," she added. It was the only thing that made sense. But what? Ronan was an angel. A dark one. Had he always been that way? What made him fallen? Zak hadn't indicated that he had any knowledge of him, but considering his memories had been suppressed for hundreds of years, maybe he hadn't dug through them enough to find the thread that linked them together.

She'd just finished her breakfast when Zak strolled in.

"How are you feeling?" Immediately crossing to her side, Zak dropped a kiss on her head before sliding into the seat next to her.

"I'm good." She clasped her hand with his, the familiar warmth sizzling through her veins at the skin-on-skin contact.

"Zak, what does that say?" She pointed to the symbols still displayed on the screen. He turned his head to look.

"Heaven on Earth." Then he frowned, looking back at her. "How did I know that?"

"I think you've got a ton of stuff buried in your subconscious that hasn't worked its way out yet. Including memories that haven't made their way to the surface."

"Care to explain?"

She repeated her theory about Ronan being immortal, that he was present when the ring and dagger were created.

"We just need you to remember. Then we'll have the upper hand."

"For a change," Cole muttered, fiddling with a coaster.

"How do I unlock the memories though? If they're even there."

"Maybe I can help. If we can get you into a meditative

state I can boost things along with my magic and you can unlock everything."

"Can't hurt to try," he agreed, "but I can tell you right now there's no way I can get all Zen with you guys watching."

"We'll do it in our bedroom," Georgia told him.

"Anytime, babe," Zak drawled.

"You wish. Mind out of the gutter, Goodwin. We've got work to do."

Upstairs Zak lay on the bed, hands beneath his head, watching as she strode back and forth at the foot of the bed, muttering to herself.

"What are you doing?" he asked.

"Just running through some stuff. I need to get this right and since I'm jump starting a meditative process I'm just running through my spells."

"You've got them all memorized?" He arched a brow, impressed.

"Yeah, ever since I fell pregnant, it's like they're there in my head. I don't need the grimoires."

"Impressive. Do the others know this?"

"No one knows. Except you. The fewer people know about me and Jelly Bean the better. I'm tired of having targets on our backs."

Zak sat up on the bed, concern on his face. "This is too much for you. Too much stress."

"Oh please, you don't think I'm used to this bullshit by now? I mean, hello, there was Marius the ancient vampire who decided I made a tasty snack, then the Hunter who killed me. I can handle this. But now, you and I are starting a family." She looked him in the eye. He got it.

Coming to stand in front of her, he cupped her face in his hands. "No, I know. I've been thinking about that too."

"I mean, I never, honestly, never cared about having kids or getting married. It was never a priority for me. I couldn't imagine putting anyone's needs before my own. But you changed all that."

"And you changed that for me."

"I'll admit, I'm scared. I'm heart-racing, pit-in-my-stomach can't breathe type of scared. Because now that I have everything I never knew I wanted. I can't have it taken away from me. I will not live with this threat hanging over our heads."

"I know, I know. You're right."

"We need to stop Ronan. I have a feeling he's behind everything. He's been in the background, pulling strings like a puppeteer."

"You think so?" Zak sounded surprised.

"I do. The awakening of Marius. Someone orchestrated that. The Hunter who was spelled to kill witches. Someone did that. We didn't really think about it at the time, but now…think about it. It's all happened for a reason. I was targeted for a reason. You were targeted for a reason."

He nodded. "To stop the prophecy."

"But it wasn't stopped. We met. Fell in love. Conceived a baby. And if we don't want to live our lives constantly in fear that someone will harm our child, we need to end this. Now."

"When did you get so brave?" Zak muttered, pulling her tight against him.

"I've always been brave!" Georgia protested. "And smart. You men just don't like to admit these things." She hugged him back, felt Jelly Bean kick, knew Zak felt the movement where she was pressed up against him. Stepping back, he placed his hands on her belly, feeling their baby move.

"You've got the smartest, bravest, most beautiful momma in the world." He spoke to her bump and Jelly Bean kicked in response.

"Come on, let's do this. Lie on the bed, close your eyes." Rubbing her back, Georgia eased down on the foot of the bed and leaned against the post. Zak stretched out on top of the covers and obediently closed his eyes.

"Take a deep breath in. And out. Keep breathing big deep breaths." She listened as he breathed, then, placing a hand on his ankle, she chanted softly, sending him into a deep meditative state. "I want you to go back, way back in your mind, back to when the ring and dagger were first created. Who was there? Look around. Who do you see?" She waited in silence, giving Zak time to travel back in time, to unravel the jumble of memories clouding his mind.

"Now I want you to wander through your memories, just let them flow. If you see Ronan, follow those memories, let them unravel."

Keeping her hand on his ankle, she sent her magic into him, giving him the power to float free in his past, unhindered. Someone had put up blocks to keep him out; together they would tear them down. She started to feel a change in him, a vibration traveling from him and up her arm. His limbs twitched and she could see his eyes moving behind his closed lids as he relived his memories. She hoped they were the ones that could help them.

An hour later his eyes flicked open and he looked at her. Lifting her hand from his ankle, she smiled at him. "Well?"

"Holy shit," he muttered, swinging his legs off the side of the bed and sitting on the edge. He clutched his head in his hands.

"Are you okay?" She moved to his side, slid her arm around his waist, and leaned into him.

"Yeah. That was…unbelievable. Enlightening. I'm a little pissed that everyone seems to have been playing with my mind." He turned to her, eyes searching hers. "Are you okay?"

"I'm fine. It didn't take as much magic as I thought. I just had to make sure I held the connection with you and you pretty much did the rest on your own."

"Good. Good." He appeared rattled and she rubbed her hand up and down his back in a soothing gesture.

"Do you want to tell me about it?" she asked, voice low.

"It's terrible. I just can't believe I didn't know this."

"Because you were deliberately blocked. Zak, none of this is or was your fault. You know that, right? Everything that happened to you, your memories being taken away—they did that for your protection. For our protection. So the prophecy could happen."

"I know, I know. But Ronan. Fuck."

"What about Ronan?"

"He's my brother."

"What do you mean, he's your brother?" Frank stood hands on hips in the conference room where they'd all gathered, a scowl darkening his face.

"Half brother to be exact. But we were brought up as brothers."

"So while you're half vampire, half angel, he's all angel? Your mom and another angel?" Kyan tried to get it clear in his head.

"That's right. He's my older brother."

"And you didn't remember him until now?"

"The memory had been conveniently blocked," Zak confirmed.

"Why?" Cole asked.

"Because Ronan has been trying to get rid of me for millennia. Only he keeps failing. If I knew it was him behind everything then I might have decided to do something about it, and he can't have that."

"But how? I don't understand."

"When my mom and dad got together, Ronan was a few years old. His dad, an angel, had disappeared, no-one knew what had become of him. Then I came along and as we grew into adults mom started to get a sense that something was off with Ronan, that he had an evil streak, but he kept it very well hidden. She began to fear for humanity, for Ronan often spoke of ruling Earth, that those who stood against him would disappear as his father had done. She knew he had to be stopped, but she couldn't bring herself to kill her own child. She loved him, despite his evil nature. She and my dad decided to create the ring and dagger as weapons that could be used against him, but she knew she had to keep the balance, between darkness and light. Hence the ring can give life, the dagger takes it away.

"I was with mom and dad when they were created, they explained it all to me, but then Ronan caught us and was furious he'd been excluded from our plans, that we were plotting against him. He went into a rage, killing mom and dad, trying to kill me, but mom had slipped the ring onto my finger as she lay dying and somehow, I survived. Ronan was banished from Heaven."

"So…were you an angel? To begin with? Were you in Heaven too?" Georgia whispered.

"No, but I could visit. I mostly lived on Earth with my dad, mom could come and go as she pleased. We were in Heaven the day the ring and dagger were created. I woke up on Earth, with no memory of my parents, the ring, the dagger, or Ronan."

"Any clue as to *why* he's doing all this?"

"Since he has no footing in Heaven, he wants to create Heaven on Earth. Get rid of the humans, populate it with angels, with Nephilim and demons to do his bidding. Become a God."

"What the hell?" Frank muttered.

"Ronan was banished from Heaven. He's never forgiven them for it."

"And he's waited all this time?"

"He couldn't find me. Couldn't find the ring, or the dagger. My parents must've put some sort of protection spell over me to keep me hidden. Protecting me even as they died. But of course, once the ring activated, I was visible."

"But he found you before then," Georgia reminded him. "He got the demons together, and they attacked you in Eden Hills. The ring didn't activate until after your home was destroyed."

"You're right," Zak admitted. "I don't know if that was coincidence or not, but yeah, he found me just as you did."

"He was too late. The prophecy was starting."

Zak nodded. "And he's been trying to desperately stop it ever since."

"Okay. Now that our minds are blown, what's the next step?" Frank asked what they were all thinking. It was all well and good that they'd discovered Ronan was Zak's brother but now what?

"I want to go and check out the warehouse again. He was cocky and arrogant enough to write 'Heaven on Earth' on the wall. There might be other clues."

"We'll come with you." Cole rose, but Zak waved him back to his seat.

"No. I'll go alone. I want you all to stay here and keep an eye on things. He's after Georgia and the baby. Killing me would be a bonus, but I'm not the main target anymore. They are. Keep them safe."

Zak teleported and the room settled into silence.

"Okay. Now what?" Cole asked.

"I say we finish getting the nursery ready." Georgia smiled, sliding her hands beneath her bump. "It won't be long before Jelly Bean is here. The least I can do is be ready."

"Great plan! What do you need?" Frank was by her side in

an instant, a hand cupping her elbow and helping her to her feet.

"I've got a stash of baby things at the farm. In the workshop, there's a wardrobe waiting for me to refurbish it. Inside are some bags and boxes of baby stuff. Can you bring them here?"

"You've got it."

"What can we do to help?" Kyan asked.

"The nursery needs another coat of paint. Zak's done the first coat, so if one of you could do that, it'd be great. The baby furniture is all stored in the workshop out the back. Once the painting is done can you bring it in? There's a dresser, a bookshelf, change table, and cot. There's also a bassinet, but that can go in my room, please."

"I'll get the painting done." Cole volunteered, heading out.

"I'll get the furniture sorted," Kyan said.

That left Aston who sat at his computer looking somewhat dejected.

"Don't worry, I have a job for you," Georgia told him. He perked up immediately. "Oh?"

"Can you make a start on creating a family tree? An illustrated one that we can have printed, framed and put on the wall?"

"Absolutely, it'll be my pleasure." He swiveled back to his computer and began typing.

With the warriors busy helping put the nursery together, Georgia made her way upstairs. Stopping outside Skye's door, she knocked softly. After a few minutes, the door cracked open.

"What?" She looked terrible. Her hair was an unwashed mess around her head and she wore an oversized T-shirt, one of Dainton's Georgia guessed, her feet bare.

"Just checking in." Georgia raised her hand to push the door further open, but Skye stopped her.

"I want to be left alone," she muttered. "I helped get Raquel, Jenna, and Leslie settled last night—they're fine by the way—but that's it. I'm done."

"The guys are putting together the nursery. I thought you might like to help? A change of scenery might be good? Give you something else to focus on."

"No, thanks. Ask the witches."

"It's not your fault, you know. If you're blaming yourself for Dainton's death."

"He was there to rescue me. You all were. I thought I could take the Nephilim. Instead, he took me and you all had to come rescue me because I'm useless. He died because of me."

"That's not true. None of this is your fault. If you want someone to blame, blame Ronan." Georgia opened her mouth to tell her sister all that they had discovered, but Skye raised her hand, stopping her.

"No. Please let me do this my own way. Please, Georgia." Shuffling back, she closed the door. Blowing out a sigh, Georgia rested her head against the door. So much pain. All she could do was be here when her little sister was ready—and pray to God she didn't do anything stupid in the meantime.

16

"The witches are in Kanurbury," Zak told Georgia on his return. Kanurbury was a smallish town a hundred miles from Redmeadows, a sleepy place that was once a bustling mining town but since the giant mining companies pulled up stakes and departed, Kanurbury was quietly slipping into obscurity, families moving away to find better jobs, better schools for their kids, a better life than one in a dying town.

"How do you know?" she asked from her position on the sofa where she'd been napping.

"Because the moron wrote it on one of the walls. His arrogance will be his undoing."

"Do you know where in Kanurbury?"

"Unfortunately, no. And I've never been there before, so I can't teleport to try and find them."

"I'm sure Aston can do some searches online to see if he can find anything. Somewhere remote where you could hold a bunch of witches against their will without anyone noticing. If we head off now, he may have found something by the time we get there?"

"That's what I was thinking," Zak agreed. "How's Skye? And the witches?"

"The witches are okay. Subdued. I've put them to work washing baby clothes and helping get the nursery set up. It's not much, but it's keeping them busy and focused on something else."

"And Skye?"

"She's in so much pain, Zak." Georgia sighed, her own heart aching at the hurt Skye was going through.

"I can help with that," Zak told her and she knew he meant with the sire bond. He could turn off her emotions, take away her pain.

"Absolutely not! This is part of living. And loving. Do not mess with her. She needs to find her own way through it. If you do something to her through the sire bond, command her to pull herself together or to forget her pain, I'll never forgive you!"

"Okay, okay, I'll leave it." He held up his hands in surrender. "Come on. Let's hit the road. If we head off now we should make Kanurbury by nightfall." Clasping her hand in his, he led her outside where Frank had two black SUVs waiting.

"How many cars do you have anyway?" Georgia suddenly asked, letting Zak boost her into the passenger seat of the front vehicle. "Six. Not counting your truck." He grinned, snapping her seatbelt in place. "I keep losing them. They get left behind when I teleport and sometimes by the time we get back to collect them, they've been stolen or torched."

"Your insurance premiums must be a bitch."

"Not insured. Too much traceable red tape. I can afford it. I'm loaded, remember?" His grin was sexy as sin as he slid behind the wheel.

"Oh yeah, that's why I agreed to marry you," she teased,

patting his knee. Their joking was interrupted by Cole and Frank climbing into the back seat.

"Where's Kyan?" Georgia asked.

"He's riding with Aston in the other car. And here, I grabbed you this." Leaning between the seats Frank handed her the dagger. Shit, how could she have forgotten it? Baby brain hits again. Jelly Bean twitched in protest.

"Thanks." She placed it across her lap, again bemoaning her lack of boots to stash the dagger in.

They pulled out, heading away from Redmeadows. The motion of the car lulled her and within minutes Georgia was asleep, head resting against the window.

THE STREET they turned down was little more than an overgrown dirt track. Pieces of broken bitumen stuck up amongst the potholes and the collapsing buildings with their broken windows peered at them in the darkness. No streetlights here, the globes had all been smashed.

Zak turned off the street and pulled up alongside a tired old building that looked like a strong gust of wind could knock it over. Aston had found what they thought they were looking for.

"Is this it?" Georgia asked, surprised.

"No. It's further down the street. I don't want to risk them hearing us, so we'll stop here and I'll go scout around. If it's safe we can get the cars a little closer. I don't want them far away in case we have to run for it." His eyes landed on her bump and she knew he was worried about her. She couldn't run as fast as she used to, and she refused to let him teleport her, terrified it would harm Jelly Bean.

"Frank, take the wheel. I'll call with the plan." Leaning over, he kissed her hard on the mouth before climbing out of the vehicle, leaving the door open for Frank to take his place. Once Frank was behind the wheel, Zak disappeared. They waited in the car in silence, all lost in their own thoughts. Georgia's most pressing thought was she needed to pee. The next? She was hungry.

As if reading her mind Frank handed her a chocolate bar. "Here," was all he said.

"Thank you." Georgia smiled, ripping the wrapper and taking a bite. "What about you guys? You all good?"

"I brought a thermos." Cole held up a blue thermos, full of heated blood. "Kyan has one as well. We'll be fine."

Frank's phone vibrated and he snatched it up from where he'd set it on the dash. "Yeah?"

"The witches are here." Zak's voice came through the phone. Frank pressed the speaker so they could all hear.

"How many?" Georgia asked.

"A lot. A real lot. Maybe a hundred?"

"Shit!" Cole swore. "How are we going to get them all out?"

"We'll worry about that once we've got Ronan and his minions out of the way."

"How many of them?" Frank asked.

"Surprisingly, not many. I think Ronan is so confident we won't find this place that he's left minimum guards here. About ten that I can see. There's some sort of machine. It appears the witches are attached to it in some way."

"What's the plan?"

"Bring the cars a little closer. Three buildings down. I'll meet you there."

Hanging up, Frank started the car, signaling to the vehicle behind them to reverse out. With their lights off they slowly crept down the street, turning down the alley three buildings down. Frank left the car idling and hopped out, spoke briefly with the car behind them, then returned.

"We're going to turn the cars around in case we need a speedy getaway," he explained as they maneuvered themselves in the narrow space. Kyan was driving the other vehicle and he parked on the other side of the driveway, so they weren't blocking each other.

Zak appeared at Georgia's door and helped her out, threading his fingers with hers as the warriors gathered around them.

"I think the key here is to turn off or preferably destroy that machine. It looks like it's draining the witches, taking their power, if we turn it off, with any luck their magic will return and they'll be able to help us."

"Aston and Cole, take the South door. Frank and Kyan take the West. Georgia and I will be behind you."

The warriors rushed off, moving at lightning speeds, while Zak and Georgia walked toward the warehouse at a slower pace.

"You don't need to stay with me," Georgia protested, feeling bad she was keeping him from his warriors.

"There is nowhere else I'd rather be than by your side," he replied, squeezing her hand.

"Do you know how corny that sounds?" She giggled.

"I do. But it's true. I misjudged the situation last time and you almost got taken. Never again. You and our baby are the most important things to me. You have to come first."

"Babe." Her heart melted at his words. Stopping, she turned and wrapped her arms around his waist. "I love you."

"I love you too, my little spitfire." Kissing her softly, he led her through the darkness to the warehouse, where they crouched beneath one of the only intact windows of the building. Rising up on her toes, Georgia peeked inside and gasped at what she saw. Two industrial lights stood on stands at either end of the warehouse, providing just enough light to see by. In the middle of the room was a large machine, shaped like a rocket and in circles expanding out from the base stood row upon row of witches, radiating outward like a shockwave. On their heads were what looked like bike helmets, all with a cable leading to the rocket-like machine.

The hairs on Georgia's arms rose in response. Oh yes. There was a lot of magic in the machine, she could feel it. Now they just needed to return it to the witches. Focusing on the women and men attached to the machine, she frowned. Some were in bad shape. What looked like blood trickled from their noses to splash down their fronts, their cheeks were hollowed, and they swayed on their feet. Near the back, she could see shapes on the floor and could only guess some of them had collapsed. Or died.

"We need to get them out," she whispered to Zak, urgency lacing her voice.

"I know. We will. How many guards do you see?"

She peered around the warehouse, focusing on the shadows. "Four. I only see four. But you said there were, what, ten?"

"About that, yeah. Stay down."

Georgia was about to drop down when she spotted Kyan directly opposite the window she was peering through. He approached on silent feet behind a demon and slit its throat, catching its body and lowering it to the floor without a sound. Glancing around, he moved forward, eyes on the next target.

"Down." Zak tugged on her hand and reluctantly she dropped down, crouching next to him. Pressing her ear to the tin of the warehouse, she listened. The odd scuffle and grunt reached her ears until Zak tapped her shoulder, drawing her attention to him.

"They've taken down the demons. It's safe to go in." Standing, he pulled her to her feet and led the way inside.

The smell was horrific and Georgia gagged.

"Some of them have died," Frank said, explaining the stench that was assailing her nostrils.

"That bastard." She cursed, weaving her way through the remaining witches. She needed to break the connection with this damn machine. The closer she got to it, the more she could feel it, a hum that made her ears vibrate and static electricity that made her hair stand on end. Each cord that was attached to individual helmets fed directly into the machine. There was no way to rip the cord out this end. What would happen if they simply took the helmets off the witches? Would it kill them? Too afraid to risk it, she decided the best way was to turn the machine off first.

"I can't find a switch of any sort." Cole met her at the base of the machine and they both looked up. It stood over two stories tall.

"How the hell do we turn it off?" Resting her palm on it, she felt the jolt of magic and knew the answer.

"Magic. The switch is magic." She breathed out, running her palm over the surface again. It felt warm to her touch. A living, breathing entity.

"Will your magic work? Can you turn it off?" Cole touched the machine as well, but it felt like cold metal to him.

"I would say Ronan is probably the only one," Georgia guessed, "but I'll give it a try. Are you ready, Jelly Bean? Momma needs your help, baby." Closing her eyes she placed both palms on the machine and sucked in a deep breath, drawing her magic up into her hands, holding it, letting it build. She felt Jelly Bean's magic swirl through her, adding to her own. Blowing out her breath, she pushed the wave of magic out, willing it into the machine, willing the machine to stop.

The backlash from the magic release forced her back and

she staggered. Zak steadied her, an arm around her shoulders.

"Are you okay?" Concern clouded his voice.

"I'm fine. Phew, a bit of a magic rush is all...did it work?" She glanced at the witches who stood around them, unmoving. Damn it. Turning back to the machine she placed her hand on it again. "The magic has stopped. But it's still inside here. It hasn't gone back to the witches."

A loud clapping from the far end of the warehouse had them all spinning around. Ronan stood there, applauding them.

"Well done. I didn't think you'd find this place. I see I have underestimated you, but don't fret, I won't do that again." His lip curled in a sneer and Georgia itched to slap it right off his face. Zak held onto her wrist, restraining her.

"Release the witches," she demanded, body trembling with anger.

"Are you sure?" Ronan arched a brow. What was he playing at? Was this a trick? A trap of some sort?

"Start taking their helmets off!" Georgia yelled, pulling free of Zak's hold and reaching for the witch closest to her, unsnapping the clasp and ripping the helmet from her head. The warriors followed suit, but they weren't fast enough. Over the noise Georgia could hear Ronan chanting and then they started to fall, blood pouring from their eyes, nose, and ears.

"No! No! No!" she screamed, frantically trying to save them, but it was no good, he'd killed them. The hum and static electricity from the machine dimmed, the magic dying with the witches. But they'd saved some, and for that she was grateful. Those whose helmets they'd snatched off were on the floor, unconscious but not dead.

She became aware of movement in the shadows, shapes lurked there, and she could feel eyes on her in the darkness.

More demons? Or Nephilim? Or both? She didn't have to wait long to find out. Nephilim. At least a dozen, possibly more. She braced herself, glad of the dagger held firmly in her hand—this time she'd be prepared, this time Ronan would pay.

The first Nephilim reached her and she waved him away with a blast of magic. She sensed another behind her and swung her arm back, piercing the Nephilim in the stomach with the dagger. She spun, driving the dagger up into his heart. His face registered surprise, then he dropped at her feet, dead. More came at her, wave after wave but her magic easily defeated them, slamming them into the floor, walls, even the roof. She used one as a bowling ball, sending it hurtling toward the others, knocking them all down with a satisfying thunk, thunk, thunk.

Between her magic and the dagger, she was holding her own, when it slipped from her grasp, slick with blood. Bending she picked it up, wiping the blood from the blade on her pant leg. Zak was suddenly at her back, blocking a blow that would have felled her, for while she was distracted with the dagger, a Nephilim had gotten too close.

"Get her out of here!" Zak shouted. Aston obeyed without hesitation. He wrapped his arms around her protectively and dragged her across the floor despite her protests.

"No!" Georgia shouted, grabbing for Zak. Blood gushed from a wound on his shoulder. She couldn't leave him.

When they reached the door she fought harder, but Aston was not budging. He had his orders and he'd see them through. Within seconds they were at the car and he was bundling her into the passenger seat. One second later he was behind the wheel and fishtailing down what used to be a road.

"We have to go back. We have to help them!" Georgia

protested, hand clenching the arm rest as Aston drove at breakneck speeds.

"No chance."

"Aston, please," she begged, "we can't lose another."

"We won't. But they need this, they need to exact their revenge. Zak is dealing with Ronan. The others are finishing off the Nephilim that Ronan brought with him."

"And the witches?" A tear trickled down Georgia's cheek and she absently wiped it away.

"We'll take the survivors to a safe place. I can't tell you anything more." Aston kept his eyes on the rearview mirror.

"Are we being followed?" she asked. He shook his head. "No. Too much chaos at the warehouse. Ronan didn't see us leave."

By the time Aston pulled up outside their home in Redmeadows, Zak and the others had returned. It was deja vu. The last time was when Dainton had been killed and Georgia couldn't shake the bad feeling she had.

"The witches?" Georgia whispered, letting Zak help her out of the car.

"At a motel in Redmeadows. We need to ward it though. I was going to go there with Skye but under the circumstances..."

"I'll do it. It's fine. And what of Ronan?"

"He got away. Again." She could hear the anger and frustration in Zak's voice. Hugging him tight, she remained silent for a moment before shifting her weight from foot to foot.

"I need to pee," she admitted ruefully, hating to ruin the moment, but with Jelly Bean sitting on her bladder, peeing had become her world.

Keeping his arm around her, Zak led her inside, waiting patiently while she dealt with her bladder, then seating her at her favorite spot at the breakfast bar.

"Hungry?" he asked. Georgia nodded. "I'm sorry. I'm always hungry and I always need to pee."

"Never apologize, babe." Zak shrugged, fixing her a sandwich and passing her a glass of juice.

"How many survived?" she asked, playing with the glass of juice, spinning it in her fingers.

"About twenty. Haven't done an official head count."

"Did you see Carol? Meghan? Jessica?" she asked hopefully.

"Sorry, it was so rushed I didn't get a good look at anyone. Ronan took off. I didn't follow. Couldn't leave the warriors. " His voice cracked and he broke off, head low, staring at his shoes. She knew he was thinking about Dainton, how he hadn't been able to save him.

"I'm sorry. About Dainton. He was a good warrior. A good friend," she told him.

"You didn't seem to think so. Not recently."

"Mom warned me Skye was going to be heartbroken. She didn't say why or what happened. I made an assumption." She shrugged. "You know what they say about assumptions."

"Yeah. I do." He blew out a breath and looked her in the eye, his own bloodshot. "I'm bloody tired." It was the first time Zak had ever shown any weakness.

Filled with concern, she slid from the stool and rounded the kitchen bench to his side, wrapping a supportive arm around him. "Go get some rest."

"We need to protect the witches," he protested though the tiredness on his face told her there was nothing he wanted more than to lie down and close his eyes. She knew the feeling.

"You rest. I'll get Frank to take me." She hated how easily she lied to him, but circumstances warranted it. He was dead on his feet, hadn't slept in days, not properly.

"Are you sure?" He took a step toward the door and halted.

She nodded, "I'm sure. Frank or one of the guys can take me. You need to rest, I need you at full strength for when we take down Ronan." It was a sound plan, only she didn't think any of the warriors were in any better shape than Zak. All of them were exhausted. She intended to drive to the motel on her own, giving Zak and his warriors their much-needed rest while she took care of protecting the rescued witches.

He looked at her for a second longer before nodding his head. She heard his footsteps heavy on the stairs. As soon as the bedroom door closed she slid from the stool and made her way to Skye's room. Eventually, her sister opened the door.

"How are you doing?" she asked.

"Mom kinda got it right," Skye responded, voice devoid of emotion.

"Kinda. I wish I'd known."

"It's not your fault," Skye muttered. Georgia knew differently. All of this was her fault. Dozens of witches died tonight because of her. Dainton died, because of her. Swallowing past the lump in her throat she dropped her hand, took a step back, away from her sister. Skye let her go, closing the door and presumably returning to bed.

The house was silent when she left. Climbing into her Ford Jailbar she turned the key in the ignition, making sure the radio was off and waited. Zak was so attuned to her he'd realize immediately that it was her truck he could hear and not Franks'. Zak slept upstairs, his own exhaustion and grief too much for even him to bear. The warriors oblivious as they too wallowed in the loss of their comrade. Slowly she eased the truck down the driveway, not flicking on the lights until she hit the road.

It was quiet in Redmeadows in the dead of night. Zero

traffic on the road. Eerie. Finally, she spotted the motel where Zak said he had left the witches. Pulling into the parking lot she killed the engine and stepped out of the truck.

"What are you doing here?" A voice spoke from the shadows of the front office.

"Geez, Rhys, give a girl a heart attack why don't you?" Sucking in a startled breath she headed toward him, making out his silhouette where he leaned against the building, one booted foot drawn up and resting against the siding.

"Sorry." He dropped his foot and stepped toward her. "You didn't answer my question. What are you doing here?"

"I need to ward this place to keep the demons from finding the witches. If they stay inside and don't use magic, they'll be fine. Step outside and all bets are off."

"Right." He nodded, falling into step beside her.

"What are you doing here?" she asked in return.

"Keeping an eye on things. Got a call from Frank. So what is Zak doing letting you out of his sight?"

"He doesn't know I'm here by myself. Dainton's death is taking its toll. He's torn apart, Rhys. Gutted. So is Skye. Fuck, they all are."

"Yeah. I bet." After all, it wasn't even a year ago when the Alpha and his wife were killed. Rhys knew all about grief and sorrow. "So what do we need to do to ward this place?"

"Their blood. I'm going to have to ward the whole building, so I'll need to mix their blood. In this." She dug around in the bag she'd slung over her shoulder and pulled out a small silver bowl. "I just need a blood sample from each of them and I'll do the rest."

"Let's do this." Leading the way, Rhys knocked on the first door. An exhausted Carol pulled it open, peering at him. "What is it?" she croaked, then saw Georgia and squealed.

"Carol?" Georgia pushed past Rhys and into the room, wrapping her friend in a hug.

"You don't know how good it is to see you!" Carol cried. She was a mess, her clothes filthy, her hair knotted.

"Are you okay? Are you hurt? Are Meghan and Jess with you?" Georgia looked around the room. Carol appeared to be the only occupant.

"Jess is in the shower." Carol nodded toward a door at the back of the motel room. "I haven't seen Meghan. I don't think she made it." The last was said in a whisper.

"I'll check the other rooms. Maybe she's in one of them." Georgia didn't want to believe Meghan was dead. There'd been too much death tonight. "What's happening? Why were we taken?" Carol asked, sitting on the side of the bed.

"*Readers Digest* version," Georgia grunted, digging around in her bag for the dagger and placing the silver bowl on the bench next to the television. "Zak has a brother, Ronan. A dark angel. He's been trying to stop me and Jelly Bean from completing the prophecy. To do that he built this machine that was draining the magic from the witches—he has a nefarious plan to steal your magic and somehow transfer it to the Nephilim. Only when we were breaking you out, he turned up and killed most of you. Right now I need to ward this building to keep you hidden and safe because I don't know what Ronan is going to do next, but since he just lost a truckload of magic that he wanted to harvest I'm betting he'll be on the hunt for more witches."

"Oh. Ah. Okay. That's…intense." Carol looked stunned and Georgia couldn't blame her. It was a fantastical story. If only it weren't true.

"I need your blood." Georgia indicated the dagger and bowl. "Not a whole lot, but I need blood from each of you to do the spell. As long as you all stay inside and don't use magic you'll be fine."

"Okay. Well, do you think someone can get us food and a change of clothes?" Carol crossed to where Georgia waited and held out her hand. Dragging the dagger across her palm Carol fisted her fingers and tilted her hand, squeezing the blood into the bowl.

"I'm on it," Rhys said from outside. "The wolves are keeping watch. I'll get supplies in too. Let us know if you need anything in particular."

"Thank you." Georgia handed her friend a bunch of tissues to stem the bleeding. "I need to keep moving to get this done before the demons come sniffing around." She apologized for not staying longer, but Carol waved her away.

"I know this isn't a social call, don't stress. Let me get Jess from the bathroom."

After Georgia had collected Jess's blood she made her way to each room, until she'd finally got them all. Zak had been right, twenty witches. Some of them in really bad shape. She healed what she could, but some of them were bordering on starvation. They needed intravenous drips and medicine she couldn't provide.

"Can you get your doctor here, or medicine person or whoever you wolves use?" she asked Rhys once she'd closed the door on the last room.

"Already got a call in. Along with a ton of good home cooked food and clothing that may or may not fit. My wolves know how to be discreet, don't worry." He stood behind her and watched as she dipped her finger in the bowl of blood and drew symbols on the doors and windows of the ten motel rooms housing the witches. With each symbol, she chanted the spell to keep them hidden.

She was rinsing the bowl and dagger clean at the garden tap next to the parking lot when the pain hit, so sharp and intense that she cried out, dropping everything.

"What is it?" Rhys was by her side in a second.

"Pain." She gasped, doubling over and panting.

"Labor?" he asked, pulling out his phone, getting ready to time contractions.

She shook her head. "No. My arm. Argh."

"Your arm? Let me see." Pushing up her sleeve, he cursed. "What the hell, Georgia?"

"It's been fine. Until now." While Ronan's mark was black against her skin it hadn't bothered her up until this point. Another wave of pain swept over her, and she clenched her teeth to stop from crying out. No need to freak out the witches with her shrieking and wailing outside their doors.

She panted. "We need to get out of here, away from the witches. If he's tracking me through this I'll lead him straight to them."

"Come on. In my truck. I'll take you home, the concealment spell should shield you there." Swinging her up into his arms, Rhys jogged to his truck and expertly buckled her into the passenger seat. Sweat bathed her face and her breath came in short pants. Her arm hurt like the devil and she felt sick. The interior light came on when Rhys jumped in and she caught a glimpse of her arm. The veins in her wrist stood out, black and stark against her almost translucent skin, spreading black poison through her body.

"Call Zak," she gasped, clutching her arm as Rhys peeled out of the parking lot, fishtailing as they sped down the highway.

"Calling the Doc first." Rhys gritted, cell phone glued to his ear, "Doubtful Zak has a cure for this, but the Doc might be able to help."

Rhys arranged for his pack doctor to meet them at Zak's house, then broke every speed limit in Redmeadows to get her home. She was in and out of it, her body heavy and sluggish, lights too bright, sounds too loud.

"Babe, what's happened?" She heard Zak's voice in her ear

but couldn't answer, finally unclenching her teeth and letting her scream shatter the night air.

"Oh God!" Skye's voice now, her touch cool against Georgia's heated skin. "Is it the baby? Is she in labor?"

"Her arm. Ronan's mark." Rhys stood back, letting Zak carry her inside and lay her on the sofa. "My pack's medic is coming. He'll be here any minute."

"What do you mean, Ronan's mark?"

"On her arm? Didn't you know?"

"We thought it was a bruise." Skye again, voice strained. "Is she going to die? Please don't let her die. I couldn't bear to lose her too."

Georgia struggled to penetrate the fog of pain, to reassure them all, but it was as if a wet heavy blanket covered her and she couldn't push through. She could hear screaming, knew it was coming from her but couldn't stop. She could feel hands pinning her down as her body convulsed, could hear everything around her but couldn't respond. She was dying. And Jelly Bean was dying with her. The mere thought of it made her cry out in anguish.

"Ssh, love. Breathe. Fight it. For me. For us. FIGHT!" She felt Zak's grip crushing her hand, then shuffling and a different hand was on hers, a different voice, one she hadn't heard before.

"This isn't good," the man said, his voice laced with sorrow. "She's been poisoned."

"There must be something you can do." Zak's voice, filled with anguish and rage, pierced her fog and she opened her eyes.

"I can slow it down." The man was busy with something in his bag and Georgia realized he must be the doctor from Rhys's pack. She looked over his head at Zak.

"It'll be okay," she whispered. The look on his face said he didn't believe her.

"Where's the kitchen? I need to mix these herbs into a tea for her. This isn't something modern medicine can fix. We need to turn to the old ways. This is old, dark magic."

Zak led the doctor to the kitchen and stayed with him, she could hear the murmur of their voices. Skye came and sat at her feet, her face pale and tear stained.

"At least I got you out of your room," Georgia teased

"You'd better get better then," Skye replied.

"Okay." Georgia smiled, as scared as she was, she had a feeling they'd get through this. Jelly Bean nudged her ribs in agreement.

"Right. Drink this. You're going to need a cup of this four times a day—it should stop the progression of the poison and help ease the current symptoms."

Easing into a sitting position Georgia accepted the steaming mug and took a sniff. Nice. It smelled like old farm —cow manure and cut grass. And she had to drink four cups of this a day? Holding her nose, she put the cup to her lips and gulped it down. Eyes watering and gasping for breath, she sat the cup on the coffee table in front of her.

"How long?" she gasped, the taste foul on her tongue.

"Until it takes effect? Not long. I've made a batch in the kitchen. One of your men is putting it in a thermos for you. I'll leave the recipe and herbs for another two batches."

"We'll need more." Zak frowned and the doctor shrugged. "That's all I have on me right now. It'll hold you for three days, maybe a bit longer. I'll come by and check on you and bring more. In the meantime, I'll see what I can find out about the mark, see if there are any other treatments."

"And the baby? Will any of this affect the baby?"

"No. As long as we can stop the poison from reaching it, the baby will be fine."

It was sobering, knowing that Jelly Bean's life was on the line with hers. Georgia already had a plan in mind if they couldn't stop the poison. She'd have to deliver Jelly Bean early; it was the only way to save her. As if reading her mind, the doctor's eyes met hers.

"How far are you?"

"Thirty-six weeks."

"Good." He nodded and she knew exactly what he was thinking—it was what she was thinking as well. Jelly Bean would be okay if delivered anytime between now and her due date. After all, she was languishing in her womb putting on weight; all her limbs and organs were already developed.

"I'll return in three days. Call me if anything changes."

"Thank you." Georgia nodded and felt like some secret message passed between them. She had a feeling he'd be returning with surgical equipment ready to do a cesarean and she was a hundred percent okay with that. She couldn't let her mind dwell on the fact that it also meant she was dying.

17

"I have a lead." Rhys stood on the doorstep, face grim. Stepping aside Georgia invited him in. The herbal cocktail the doctor had created was doing its job. She felt relatively okay. The black veins on her arm had stopped progressing, but they hadn't faded—a reminder that she was on borrowed time.

"The guys are in the front room," she told him, following as he turned left from the foyer and into the large room that should have been a sitting room only they'd turned it into more of a conference room with a massive table and Aston's computer set up in one corner.

"You have news?" Zak looked up from where he'd been pouring over some old parchment.

"A possible lead. One of the wolves told me about an angel they came across in Kanurbury. Not Ronan, a different angel."

"I didn't know we had this many angels on Earth," Cole muttered, shaking his head.

"There are several hundred, if not thousands. I can feel them," Zak said.

"Feel them? How?" Georgia asked.

"Like an energy. Always there."

"Can you use it to track them?"

"If I could, don't you think I'd have done that already?" His words were abrupt and she reared back in her seat at his tone. The regret on his face was immediate. "Sorry. Sorry. This is not your fault and I shouldn't take it out on you." He ran both hands over his head and blew out a breath.

"You're wrong," Georgia said softly, eyes swimming. "All of this is exactly my fault. I started everything, triggered everything. Thanks to me all these people are dead, not just Dainton and the witches, but the Alpha and his wife, my aunt and her coven, my parents, grandparents."

"No. You can't take all of that on board." Zak shook his head. "No one knew who the prophecy referred to. It didn't have your name. No, Ronan started this whole chain of events, he's to blame, not you. You're a victim like everyone else."

Frank cleared his throat. The conversation was moving into dangerous territory. "Let's leave the blame game at the door, eh? What else can you tell us about this angel, Rhys?"

"That my guy bumped into him at The Grove bar in Kanurbury, and he got the distinct impression that this particular angel likes to drink. A lot. It's a stab in the dark, but I say we go stake out the bar, see if we can find him."

"Do we have a name?"

Rhys shook his head. "Nope. Description only, brown hair, hazel eyes."

"That describes half the population. Not a whole lot to go on."

"Remember angels are a pretty good-looking bunch. I'd say just look for a guy with brown hair who looks like he could be on the cover of a magazine. Most likely that's our guy."

"Good point."

"I want to go," Georgia told them.

Zak shook his head. "No way. Too dangerous. Ronan is out there."

"Sweetheart, Ronan knows exactly where I am." She held up her arm with the black veins. "He doesn't need to find me, as far as he's concerned I'm no longer a threat."

"What if he's pissed you've stopped the poison and decides to simply kill you on the spot?"

"You think I'm helpless? Defenseless? Have you forgotten it was you who trained me to fight?"

"He got you once, he can get you again."

"The same can be said for any of you." She eyeballed them all around the table. "He got Dainton. We never thought any of you were at risk. Will that stop you from fighting, from tracking him down and dealing with him once and for all? No, of course not. Stop wrapping me in cotton wool. I am not going to sit here and do nothing."

"Think of the baby if not of yourself!" Zak stood up so fast his chair toppled over backward, anger radiated from him in waves. Georgia rose to her feet in a more leisurely manner. She knew he was angry because he was scared. She understood.

"I will not put myself or our baby in harm's way. If I didn't think I could protect myself I would not leave this house. Ever. Plus I'm not saying I'm going to The Grove on my own. One of you will be with me. Jelly Bean and I are the prophecies—we have power—it's not going to be this easy for Ronan. The fight is far from over."

"What do you mean?"

"Just that I have a feeling. A very strong feeling."

"A vision?"

"No. Just a sense. Even with his stupid mark, I'm still here. Each problem he throws our way, we're finding solutions. That's gotta make him frustrated, right? He's going to make a wrong step. We need to be there when he does."

18

The fries at The Grove were to die for. In Georgia's opinion anyway. Shoving another in her mouth she chewed and scanned the crowd. Slim pickings for a Friday night, but the place was a bit of a dump and she figured most people had someplace better to be. The Grove was the type of bar you visited to get shit faced drunk and not be bothered by other people.

It was her second night here. They'd finally agreed on a plan. Split up, travel in pairs and scope out all the drinking places in Kanurbury. Of course, there was the danger the angel they were looking for had moved on, but Zak seemed reasonably confident the angel was in the town. He could feel the angelic energy. Of course, it could just mean he was picking up on Ronan. Zak was scoping out Redmeadows, teleporting to various pubs, clubs and drinking holes. He'd join them here later.

"There." Rhys nudged her elbow and she glanced up. They'd taken a corner booth where they had a good view of the bar. At the door, a man strolled in, blue jeans, black leather jacket, brown hair tied up in a man bun, aviator glasses. He was gorgeous. Jaw dropping, drool in your fries gorgeous.

"Oh yeah. That's him." Placing her palms on the cracked Formica table top, she got ready to slide out of the booth when Rhys turned to her, brows raised.

"Uh yeah, I don't think so. Wait here. I'll bring him over," Rhys reminded her. They had a deal. She could come if she stayed off her feet and out of trouble. She'd almost laughed out loud at that—trouble seemed to follow her around. It had turned up on her doorstep one day in the shape of Zak Goodwin and had never left.

She watched as Rhys approached the angel. They spoke and the angel shrugged, glancing across at her before looking back at Rhys and nodding. Rhys waited while the man ordered a beer and then led him to their booth.

Rhys introduced them. "Georgia, this is Marcus. Marcus, Georgia."

"Hear you've got yourself in a spot of trouble." Marcus removed his sunglasses to reveal mesmerizing hazel eyes.

"Just a smidge." Georgia lifted her hand and held her finger and thumb an inch apart. Marcus chuckled, then frowned when her sleeve slid down her arm, revealing the black veins.

"Marked all right," he muttered, capturing her wrist, his big fingers gentle as he examined the mark on her wrist.

"What can you tell us about it?" Rhys asked, body tense, ready to spring at any sign of trouble.

"You can relax, wolf. I mean you and the witch no harm." Marcus didn't bother to raise his eyes from her wrist. He pressed his thumb directly over the mark and Georgia felt a strange tingling.

"What are you doing?" she asked, tugging lightly. His grip tightened but didn't hurt.

"Testing. I can't remove it. Did get some of the toxins out

though. And the herbs you've been taking are doing a good job, but the longer you take them, the less effective they'll be."

"So how do we get the mark off?"

"Kill the angel who put it on." His response was immediate.

"That's the only way?"

"Unless he removes it voluntarily, which, knowing Ronan, is doubtful."

"So you know Ronan?"

Marcus drained his beer, wiped his mouth on the back of his arm, and frowned at the glass on the table.

"As useless as soda," he muttered, beckoning the waitress over. The woman practically sprinted to their table, pushing her chest out she stood close to Marcus.

"What'll it be, sugar?" she purred. Georgia sighed. This is how women acted around Zak.

"Bring me a bottle of whiskey and a glass."

"Oh, we don't usually—" she began, but Marcus cut her off by wrapping his fingers around her wrist and tugging her down so he could whisper in her ear. Heaven only knows what he said, but it worked. A blush colored her cheeks and she smiled in delight.

"Coming right up." She hurried off, not even checking if Georgia and Rhys needed anything.

"Back to Ronan," Georgia said. "You know him?"

"I do. He gave me this." Easing an arm out of his jacket he showed them the scar running from elbow to wrist.

"How? Surely you'd heal."

"The bastard got his hands on the Devil's Sword. Don't know how. Just know that he almost took my head off with it and this wound took weeks to heal."

"The Devil's Sword?" Georgia asked.

"As the name suggests, a sword created in the fires of hell.

It can kill any creature. Angel, demon, vampire, you name it —there isn't anything that sword can't take care of."

"A powerful weapon."

"Indeed. But I suspect he no longer has it. Hell does not give up its secrets easily and I would imagine the sword was retrieved quickly."

"Yet they didn't kill Ronan for taking it."

"He would have tricked someone else into doing it for him. That's how he operates. He doesn't risk his own neck. He'll convince you to take the risk and then sacrifice you to whoever's wrath he's triggered."

"Is that what happened? To you? Were you and Ronan partners?"

They were interrupted with the waitress returning, a bottle of whiskey and a glass, just as he'd ordered. He poured himself a full glass and tossed it back. The rumors were true: this angel really liked his drink.

"A partnership of sorts, I suppose. I thought we were friends. Turns out he was using me to get to someone else."

"Is that when he tried to kill you?"

Marcus nodded. "Correct."

"Can I ask...why are you in Kanurbury? Is it because of Ronan?"

Marcus shrugged. "I've been tracking him for a while, keeping my distance though. I'm curious what he's up to. He's always had some crazy scheme going on and I could never work out to what purpose."

"So you don't know he's trying to create Heaven on Earth?"

"What? That's insane." Marcus snorted, taking another mouthful of whiskey. "Are you serious?"

"Deadly. He's got some scheme to get rid of the humans, or at least control them in some way and he'll rule the Earth and the Nephilim and demons will help him keep order."

"Crazy bastard." Marcus shook his head. "What about you? He's marked you, clearly, wants you out of the way. Why?"

"Because I'm the prophecy. The witch and her offspring who will bring about the dawn of a new power."

"Ahhh. I've heard whispers about you." His eyes dropped, searching for her pregnant belly, but it was hidden from view by the table top.

"Don't even think of betraying us," Rhys growled, the rumble deep in his voice intimidating.

"Relax, wolf. I'm proposing to join you. I have a score to settle with Ronan. In the past, the odds have always been in his favor, but this time, I'm thinking the odds are stacked against him and I sure as hell wanna piece of that."

Georgia and Rhys looked at each other, then back at Marcus.

"You know if you betray us Zak will kill you," Georgia told him.

"Wait—you're with Zak? He's the baby daddy?" Marcus was incredulous. "This keeps getting better and better."

"You know Zak?"

"Know of him. Angel and vampire. Real powerful magic that the silly bastard doesn't use. If only he knew."

"Knew what?"

"He could take Ronan out like that"—Marcus snapped his fingers—"with his magic. None of this running around hunting him down bullshit."

"But he can't control his magic," Georgia protested. "He risks destroying the earth if he uses it."

"And who do you think planted that seed in his head?" Marcus waited while she mulled it over.

"Ronan," she breathed.

"Exactly." Marcus barked out a laugh. "I've gotta meet this man of yours. I'm in, cross my heart I will not be betraying you." He mimicked drawing a cross over his chest. "Give me your phone."

Georgia handed it over and watched as he typed something in it and passed it back. Looking down at the screen she couldn't stop the grin. *Marcus the Magnificent* and a cell number were now added to her contacts.

"I've got a little *fun* planned for this evening, but give me a call when y'all work out what you're doing."

Marcus stood, grabbed his whiskey bottle and glass and headed to the bar. Sliding onto a vacant stool he proceeded to chat up the bartender, much to the waitresses' distress if the look on her face was anything to go by.

An alcoholic angel. Just what they needed.

SKYE PULLED Georgia to one side, her expression urgent. "I was going through our grimoire and found something… concerning." Finally, she'd come out of her room. Raquel, Jenna, and Leslie had been relocated to the motel with the other witches. It was easier to keep them safe if they were all together.

"Oh?" Georgia frowned. She hadn't spent too much time reading their family grimoire since all the spells she needed were already in her head, thanks to the thousands of witches' magic she'd absorbed when she'd freed them from the Hunter's prison. "A spell?" she asked Skye, confident it wouldn't be the earth-shattering news Skye thought it was.

"No. Not a spell. A warning. Well, given that witches and vampires have not always gotten along, it was probably meant as a warning when it was written."

Now she had Georgia's attention. Along with spells, the grimoire also contained information on different species, types of demons, artifacts. It was a veritable encyclopedia for witchcraft.

"What is it?"

"It says that if you kill a vampire, all the vampires he's sired will die with him. Or her."

"Shit." She frowned, that hadn't been what she was expecting at all. "So if Ronan—or anyone really—kills Zak… we all die."

"Yes," Skye whispered. "We need to tell Zak."

Georgia frowned. This was big news, and given Zak had been walking the Earth for thousands of years, surely he'd have been aware of this little loophole when it came to sired vampires. Or was it one of the memories Ronan had tampered with? Ronan didn't have to worry about defeating Zak's warriors, he just needed to take out one vampire: Zak himself, and the rest would fall.

Rubbing her forehead, she closed her eyes. There was a solution to every problem, and this one lay in magic, she was sure of it. She opened her mind and the witches bombarded her with spells, brews, and potions that could help. Wrinkling her nose in concentration, she sifted through their suggestions until she hit upon the perfect spell. A spell that would sever the sire bond. All she needed to do was convince Zak it was the right path.

ZAK CROSSED TO THE WINDOW, placed his palm against the glass, and peered outside. As much as he loved Georgia with all his heart, some days she drove him to distraction. Today was one of those days. More talk of breaking the sire bond between him and Skye. He knew she disliked the bond they had, that she thought he was controlling Skye and taking away her free will, but it wasn't like that. The bond was primal. A natural occurrence between a vampire and their nest.

"You really want me to break the bond with your sister, don't you?" he muttered, watching her reflection in the glass.

"I've wanted that ever since I found out about it, I won't lie," she replied, feet planted, hands on hips, ready to butt heads with him. He smiled to himself, loving her spirit. Shaking his head, he turned to face her, crossing his arms over his chest.

"And this latest fairy tale you've *'discovered'* says if I die, all vampires I've sired die with me. Where did you find that work of fiction?" His words came out more condescending than he'd intended and he winced at the flare of anger in her eyes.

"Skye found it in our family grimoire." She mimicked his actions, crossing her own arms across her chest, refusing to budge. She looked adorable and he bit back a smile. Laughing at her would not go down well so he schooled his face into a frown.

"You're forgetting one thing," he told her.

"And what's that?"

"I'm a hybrid. I'm also part angel. There's nothing to say the sire bond will affect any of you."

"Bullshit. Your sire bond has been in full effect since you turned Skye. She blindly follows your wishes. You can summon each other with a thought. That's not your angelic powers coming into play, that's all vampire. The bond is real. And if the bond is real, it can be broken."

"You know how to break it?" He shouldn't be surprised. She usually had a solution to whatever obstacle was in her way. Only this time, it was personal. It was about him and the bond he shared with his warriors—and Skye. It was intimate and special, and while he knew Georgia disliked it immensely, it was part of his vampire world. What she was asking, to have him break the bond, was no small request.

"I know a spell." She dropped her arms and crossed to him. Resting her hands on his chest, she peered into his face. "You can't tell me you'd be prepared to risk it. That if, heaven forbid, Ronan killed you, that you'd risk all of us? Because even though we don't think I'm a vampire anymore, we haven't tested that theory and you did turn me, so technically you're my sire. Think about it. Ronan is stealing the witches' magic because he needs it for something big—you. He needs to get rid of you. He knows you'll never let him turn Earth into his own twisted version of Heaven, that you'll stop him."

"Ronan is trying to stop the prophecy," he corrected her.

She inclined her head in agreement. "Yes, that's part of it. But tied up in all of that is you. If you and I weren't a couple, if you weren't the father of my child, you would still be an obstacle that Ronan needs to deal with. Now it's even more imperative since you're protecting me. You're not just a nuisance to Ronan, you're keeping him from what he desperately wants. He will kill you for it."

Looking down into her green eyes, awash with concern for him, his heart softened. He knew she wouldn't let this go, that she was like a dog with a bone. Tenacious. He just wasn't fond of being on the receiving end. With a sigh he slid his hand around her neck, cupping her nape.

"I'm not agreeing with you," he began, rubbing his thumb along her bottom lip when she opened her mouth to protest, "but I will get Aston to look into it, see what he can find out. You are right, this does affect all of us and any action we take has to be agreed to by everyone."

He knew she wanted to argue, could see the cogs turning in her pretty little head, but then she nodded in agreement. She wrapped her arms around his waist and leaned into him, resting her head on his chest. This was where she belonged, in his arms. He returned her embrace, grinning when she practically purred when he rubbed his hands along her back, half caress, half massage.

"You're distracting me," she accused, lifting her head to look at him.

"You distract me just by walking into a room," he replied, dropping a kiss on her mouth. "But you're right, time for distractions later." He playfully swatted her behind. "Let's go talk to Aston and get to the bottom of this. Then we can decide what to do."

19

"The girls are correct." Aston addressed the warriors as they sat around the table in the front room. "The sire bond is real, and if a vampire dies, all those he has sired die too."

"Why haven't I heard of this before?" Zak demanded. He'd been quietly confident the information Skye had unearthed was not true.

"Two scenarios. It could be as Georgia suggested, that if Ronan tinkered with your mind quite extensively, this would be something he would like to keep hidden from you."

"And the second scenario?"

"The vampires themselves would not want this to be common knowledge. Think about it. If you could trace a line of vampires back to the originals, then killing that original could kill thousands of vampires in one fell swoop."

"But killing an original is no easy feat," Cole pointed out.

"No, it's not. But that's not to say it can't be done."

The room fell silent, each lost in their own thoughts. It seemed Ronan was always one step ahead of them. He knew if he killed Zak, not only would it eliminate the warriors, but

Georgia and the baby too. But he needed Georgia, for now anyway, to steal her magic. He'd marked her, not killed her. The mark hadn't triggered immediately, he'd set it into action when she'd rescued the witches and drained the magic he had managed to steal. Yet she wasn't dead. Not yet. He needed her alive, but powerless.

"We spoke of the solution earlier." Georgia broke the silence. "That we—I—can break the sire bond with a spell. Are you in agreement?"

"What would it mean for us?" Kyan asked, rubbing his hand across his face.

"It would mean the return of your free will."

"That is not what the sire bond is about, Georgia," Zak cut in, anger tightening his voice. "Men, you know you have always had free will. I would never ask you to do anything I would not be prepared to do myself. I would never keep you by my side if you did not wish to be here."

"That is true." Frank nodded.

"Okay, okay." Georgia held up her hands. "Let's not get all fired up."

"Easy for you to say," Zak grumbled, but he sat back in his seat. "Continue. Explain to them what will happen."

"Look, nothing much is going to change," she reassured them. "Yes, the intimate connection with Zak will be severed —and I appreciate most of you have had that connection for a long time. You won't be able to summon him with a mere thought. And vice versa. He won't be able to give you orders through his mind; it will all need to be verbal. But that's it. You'll still be a unit, a team, a family."

"I think we should vote," Skye said quietly. "We are a family and this affects us all. And Georgia, you'll need to respect that if we decide to keep the sire bond intact, that it is our decision, that it's what we want."

"Majority rules?" Georgia asked. She wasn't happy, but

they were right. This wasn't just about what she wanted. If they truly wanted to stay sired to Zak, then she had to accept it, even if she didn't agree with it. And they'd need to make sure Ronan kept his distance. After all, Zak's brother had this knowledge as an ace up his sleeve. There had to be a reason he hadn't used it yet.

"Majority rules," Zak agreed. "Show of hands, who thinks we should break the sire bond?"

One by one the warriors raised their hands.

"Unanimous," Zak announced, voice devoid of emotion.

"It's not that we don't want to be a part of this family," Cole began, "but because we'll be stronger without it. It's a weakness, one Ronan is going to exploit at some point. This way, we'll be prepared."

"Nor is it because I would not die for you," Kyan added, nodding his head in agreement, "because I would. But this is all happening for a reason. The prophecy is unfolding and we need to do everything we can to see that it reaches fulfillment. This is part of the journey."

"It's okay, brothers." Zak shrugged. "I know your decision is not about love or loyalty." He looked at Georgia, eyebrow raised. "Now what? What do you need for the spell?"

"The spell itself is pretty straightforward, but the main ingredient I need might be a tad tricky to procure."

"And what is that?"

"The blood of an un-sired vampire." Silence greeted her words. Zak looked at her, digesting what she'd said, then he nodded.

"You need a natural born," he stated. "Not a rogue vampire, but one that has never been sired at all. Like me."

"Yes, but I can't use you because you're the one we're breaking the bond with. We need another. Are there any more originals? Because if there aren't, we're screwed."

Again the group settled into an uneasy silence. Where would they find an un-sired original vampire?

"MARCUS THE MAGNIFICENT AT YOUR SERVICE!" Marcus bowed low, then staggered, catching the doorframe to right himself.

"Are you drunk?" Georgia sighed in resignation, opening the door wider to allow the stupefied angel entry.

"Define drunk?" Marcus muttered, sashaying across the room to slump in an armchair.

"Inebriated. Pissed," Georgia supplied, closing the door, whispering *"pallio zeli"* to cloak the house and its occupants.

"Oh well, yes. That I am," Marcus agreed, his roguish grin designed to wet the panties of any woman he bestowed it upon.

"Rein it in, angel," Zak growled, moving up to Georgia, wrapping his arms around her.

"Can't help it," Marcus sighed dramatically. "It's my natural charm and angelic heart that has the ladies swooning."

"Not this one," Georgia pointed out.

"You do seem to have an unusual immunity." Marcus shifted his hazel gaze to the man behind her. "The guard dog helps."

"Hey!" Zak protested, oofing when Georgia elbowed him in the ribs.

"He's baiting you. He loves this game. Let's not buy into it, hmmmm?"

"You called. I came. Have you found Ronan yet?" Marcus sobered, leaning forward, elbows on knees, eyes suddenly sharp.

"No. That's not why I called." Settling onto the sofa, Zak

by her side, she explained the situation to Marcus. "We need to find an original vampire. Specifically, we need a sample of their blood. Since Zak's memory has more holes than Swiss cheese, he's not of much help on this one. Sorry, babe." She squeezed Zak's hand in apology.

"Ronan took all the good stuff, eh?" Marcus nodded, then looked around the living room. "Got anything to drink?"

"You want more? I can smell you from here." Georgia pinched her nose for emphasis.

"Focus," Zak snapped, eyes flashing at the angel sniffing the air like a bloodhound.

"Geez, okay. Chill. Original vampire, you say. Let me think." Slumping back, he rested his head on the back of the chair and closed his eyes. Seconds ticked by.

"You'd better not have fucking fallen asleep," Zak warned, voice edged in steel.

"Did I not just tell you to chill?" Marcus muttered, not opening his eyes. "I'm thinking. Now shush."

After another five minutes passed in silence, Marcus's eyes sprung open and he focused them on Georgia.

"You have something?" she asked, leaning forward.

"Hmmm?"

"Tell me you did not just have a micro-sleep!" She sighed in exasperation, shaking her head.

"Gotcha!" Marcus chuckled, not moving from his relaxed slouch. "I think I know who you need. Last I heard she was still active."

"She?"

"Aurora. An original vampire as requested."

"What do you mean, still active?"

"Most of the originals are sleeping these days. I'd say if you've been around for thousands of years you'd get a bit bored with the whole immortality thing as well."

"How many originals are there?"

"Dunno. Half a dozen, I suppose." Marcus shrugged. "Now about that drink?"

"Fine." Georgia started to struggle to her feet, but Zak pulled her back down. "Sit. I'll get the lush a drink."

"Are insults really necessary?" Marcus pouted, feigning hurt.

"Where can we find Aurora?" Georgia asked while Zak fixed the angel a whiskey.

"No idea." Accepting the glass from Zak, Marcus downed it in one gulp, holding the glass out for a refill. Snatching it from his hand without a word, Zak obliged. The angel was helping them after all. If they had to pay him in whiskey, so be it.

"How can we find her?" Georgia twisted to look at Zak where he stood at the bar behind the sofa.

"A locator spell?" he guessed.

She shook her head. "That wouldn't work. I need something of hers for a locator spell to work."

"Maybe I can help with that," Marcus chirped, a sexy grin dimpling his cheeks.

"Oh?"

"It was a while ago, but Aurora and I crossed paths."

"Crossed paths as in…?"

"Hooked up. Did the dirty. The vertical tango. Bumped uglies."

"I got it, I got it!" Georgia cut him off. "No need for details."

"Are you sure? Cos she was smoking hot."

"I wouldn't have thought angels and vampires were attracted to each other," Georgia muttered, watching as Zak handed Marcus his second whiskey before returning to sit beside her, threading his fingers with hers.

"Are you kidding me? Two supernatural species, almost impossible to injure? Hottest sex ever!"

Shaking her head, Georgia looked at the gorgeous angel with his man bun slightly askew, his hazel eyes with his impossibly dark lashes sweeping against his cheeks. Yeah, she could see how a vampire would be enticed to roll in the sheets with him.

"Careful," Zak grumbled, fingers tightening around hers. She looked at him and winked. While she could appreciate Marcus's charms, she had no urge to take him for a ride, so to speak.

"You said you had something of hers?" Georgia prompted.

"Yeah. She left me a little souvenir." Marcus grinned at the memory and Georgia knew just what it was that Aurora had left behind.

"She left her underwear behind, didn't she?" She moaned when Marcus nodded with great enthusiasm. "And you kept them?"

"Of course. I have a collection."

"You're such a slut." Georgia chuckled. Marcus wasn't concerned in the slightest at her opinion of his promiscuity.

"I'm a lover, not a fighter," he agreed, winking at her.

"I don't want to know the details, or where you keep your souvenirs or anything really," Georgia said, "but—god, I can't believe I'm saying this—can I borrow them? For the locator spell."

"Sure. You can keep them if you want." Marcus grinned, his innuendo clear.

"Yeah, no. Won't be needing to keep them." Georgia shuddered in mock revulsion, although to be honest, the idea of having to use another woman's panties in a spell was pretty revolting in itself.

Easing his long body to his feet, Marcus stretched, his shirt riding up to reveal abs and a trail of hair leading beneath his waistband. She had a feeling his movements were all contrived, deliberate intent to garner the interest of the opposite sex.

"Enough. Go get your souvenir, angel." Zak grabbed him by the arm and dragged him to the front door, practically throwing him out.

"Hey!" Marcus protested, but Zak slammed the door in his face.

Rising to her feet Georgia padded over to Zak, sliding her arms around his waist. "It's okay, babe, don't be jealous. He'll never be as hot as you," she reassured him. She knew what jealousy felt like, had felt its sting when Veronica had tried to derail their relationship in the early days.

20

Marcus returned with his souvenir, Aurora's underwear, but quickly departed. Apparently, he had a hot date that he didn't want to be late for. Georgia gingerly accepted the sealed plastic bag, a green satin G-string clearly visible inside.

Aston printed out a world map and spread it on the conference table. A candle held the map in place at each corner and with a snap of her fingers the flames flickered to life. Taking the underwear from the plastic bag, she clenched it in her fist and with her dagger, nicked her wrist, holding it over the map. Droplets of blood formed before her wound healed itself.

"*Quid quaeris, ex dominus signum, invenietis est magicae,*" she chanted, then waited. Sure enough, the drops of blood began to move, finally pooling in one place. Paris, France.

"Aston, print out a map of Paris. I'll re-do the spell, get us as close as we can to her location."

Zak cleared away the first map, putting the new one in its place as soon as Aston had printed it out. Georgia lit the candles and repeated the spell and they watched as the blood zeroed in on a street, a hotel.

"That's as good as it's going to get," Georgia muttered.

"Well done, babe, that's perfect. It's all I need. I'll find her, don't worry."

"You have the vial?"

"Right here." Zak held up the empty vial, tucking it securely in the pocket of his jacket. It was easier if he went alone. He'd visited Paris many times, and teleporting across the world would take him seconds. "Stay safe." He kissed her, hard, then disappeared.

"Well, that was kinda anti-climactic." Aston laughed. He was right. They were all keyed up to go and find an original vampire; instead, they were left sitting here, waiting. Only there was one thing Georgia could do while she waited.

Heading upstairs she knocked on Skye's door. While her sister was doing her best to return to a normal life, Georgia knew she was still hurting, badly. It would take her time to get over Dainton's death, and Georgia had discovered a way to help her.

"Yeah?" Skye opened the door.

"Oh good. You're still awake. Can I come in?" Georgia asked.

Holding the door open, Skye waved her arm. "Sure. What's up? How did the locator spell go?"

"It worked. Aurora's in France. Zak is there now. Hopefully, he can convince her to give us a vial of her blood."

"Good. That's good." Skye sank onto the side of her big plush bed. "So what's up?" She cocked her head, curious as to why Georgia had sought her out.

"I know it's tough when someone dies suddenly, unexpectedly, and you don't get a chance to say goodbye let alone tell them the things you've been meaning to tell them."

Georgia sat next to Skye and held her hand. "I've found a way for you to spend a little time with Dainton."

"You can bring him back?" Skye squeezed her hands so tight Georgia winced.

"No. Not back. I can bring his essence here for a little while. But it's a one-off thing. The spell will only work once."

"So…his ghost you mean?"

"Sort of, yes. You can see and hear each other, but he's not corporeal. Not physical. You can't touch him. So my question is, do you want me to do the spell for you? Or is it better for you not to see him?"

"How long? How long would he be here?"

"A couple of hours."

"So I can share the time with the others? It's not just me who will see him? Hear him?"

"He'll be confined to one space, but yes, if you want they can come here."

"How does it work?"

"I create a candle containing his essence. I cast the spell and when I light the candle, he'll appear. As soon as the candle extinguishes, he'll be gone. For good. He can only move as far as the candles glow while he's here."

"Yes. Let's do it. Thank you!" Skye hugged her tight, and Georgia hugged her back. She was glad she'd asked the other witches about it.

"I'll get the candle ready. You go tell the others, choose a location. I'd suggest here in your room so you can have some privacy."

"What about Zak?"

"It's going to take me about an hour to get the candle ready. He'll probably be back by then, or if he's not, we can wait if you like. It's up to you—I'm doing this purely for you."

"Okay. Thank you. Ummm, well we'll see, once the candle is ready we'll decide."

"Okay."

Georgia walked down the hall to her own room. She had preparations to do. Inside the dresser Zak had brought over from her farmhouse, Georgia kept her supplies. When Dainton had died, she'd cut a scrap of material from the shirt he'd been wearing when he'd been killed. The square of fabric was covered in his blood. It was the essence she needed for the candle. She hadn't known it at the time, but the witches within her must have been guiding her, making sure she'd have what she'd need for the spell.

In the bathroom, she flicked the bath taps on and sprinkled a mixture of herbs and powder into the water. She needed to cleanse herself, remove all traces of other essences from her body. Since she'd just done a spell to locate Aurora, she needed to make sure the vampire's essence was well and truly scrubbed or the spell for Dainton might fail.

Leaning back in the tub, hair piled on top of her head to keep it dry, she allowed herself to soak and relax for a few minutes. Her mind drifted, to Ronan and the demons hunting them. She'd cloaked the house and warded against demons. She and Jelly Bean should be safe, but she knew she was taking a risk each time she used her magic. If Ronan got a whiff of it, he could turn up. She needed to break the sire bond before that happened. And once the bond was broken she'd be able to protect Zak too. It was too difficult for her to cast a protection spell on him now, since it would encompass all the warriors, and would drain her magic too quickly. She'd tried previously and the spell had only held for an hour.

Stroking her hands idly over her belly she hummed a lullaby her mother had sung to her as a child. Jelly Bean kicked and wriggled, making her pleasure known.

"Soon, bubba, soon. Just let Momma sort out these pesky demons and Daddy's brother. Then we can meet, okay? Can you hold on that long?" Jelly Bean kicked again and Georgia took it as a yes.

All too soon the water cooled, forcing her out of the bath. Drying herself, she dressed in leggings and a white button-down blouse that flowed around her upper body. In bare feet, she stood at the dresser in the bedroom, placed the scrap of fabric over the black candle, held her hands over both, and chanted, *"Take essential. Fac enim vitae."* Over and over she chanted and slowly the candle changed color, from black to a deep red, finally to a rose hue. The scrap of fabric melted into the candle, becoming one with the wax. Dainton's essence was now inside. The final step was to invoke his presence via the candle.

"BABE, it's not what you think!" Zak protested, sighing when she dodged his hands, storming past him to rush downstairs.

"You think? Pray tell, Zak, just how did her lipstick come to be not only on your collar but your skin? Hmmm?" Flinging open the back door she didn't wince when it slammed against the house, although the warriors inside covered their ears. They'd all split when Zak had returned and Georgia had caught a whiff of the scent of the original vampire on him. All over him. She'd seen red. Her dagger was still embedded in the wall of their bedroom.

"Clauseruntque," she commanded. The door slammed shut, just missing Zak's nose.

"Babe, come on," he pleaded, "you know I don't need doors." He materialized on the other side and continued following her outside. She crossed the back lawn to the workshop he'd built for her. Inside was a boxing bag, similar to the one hanging in the workshop at her farm.

Whipping her blouse over her head she stood in leggings

and bra, feet bare, and pulled on her boxing gloves, tugging the binding with her teeth until the Velcro was as tight as she could get it. Then she laid into the bag, fists flying.

She'd always had a temper, a very quick temper that led her into a lot of trouble in her younger years. Now she learned to channel it, and the quickest release was physical activity. Punching something was very therapeutic and right now she wanted to punch Zak and Aurora. The bitch. She could smell her, hell, her scent was so strong she could practically taste her, on him.

"I needed her blood. I did what I had to do." Zak stood in the doorway, wary of approaching any further. She'd already thrown her dagger at him and if it wasn't for his lightning fast reflexes he'd be pinned to the wall in their room right now.

"Including sleeping with her?" One two, one two, she jabbed at the bag. It squeaked and groaned under the barrage.

"I did not sleep with her," he protested. "I swear, Georgia, I didn't. I love you, I would never cheat on you—never."

"Then it seems we are at an impasse because that lipstick didn't get all over you by accident."

"Okay look, she came on to me. Tried to seduce me. I said no."

"But you let her get pretty close. Her lips were on you, Zak. ON YOU!" Punch, punch, punch. Sweat covered her skin and she was puffing. Her rage and hurt burned through her veins until she felt like she'd combust.

Suddenly his arms were around her, pinning hers to her sides. He'd snuck up behind her while she'd been distracted with her fury. She roared in outrage, throwing her head back trying to head butt him into releasing her.

"Calm down." He cursed, evading her attack. "You'll hurt yourself."

"I'll hurt you, asshole!" she bellowed, vibrating in his arms. How could he do this to her? How could he? Tears streamed down her cheeks, but they only made her angrier.

"Let me go." She seethed, wriggling in his grasp, trying to stamp on his feet even though hers were bare and would do zero damage.

"Not until you calm down," he gritted out.

"I can't when you're rubbing her scent onto me! Get away from me. Get away!" She screamed at him and he could hear the pain in her voice.

She was right. He did smell like Aurora, and he suspected that had been the original vampire's intent when she'd pouted at him after he refused her offer. She'd agreed to give him her blood and when he'd reached out for the vial she'd pounced on him, rubbing herself on him, dragging her lips over his neck, nipping at him, tearing open his shirt and sending the buttons flying. He'd flung her off and teleported home, but the damage had been done. To all intents and purposes, it did look like he'd gotten intimate with Aurora in exchange for her blood.

"I'm sorry," he whispered, pressing his mouth against hers despite her protests, then he teleported away, leaving Georgia a crying mess. Sinking to her knees, she puffed and sobbed, sweat and dirt sticking to her skin.

MINUTES LATER ZAK WAS BACK, showered and dressed in jeans and a T-shirt, all smell of Aurora erased. Sinking to the ground behind Georgia, he pulled her into his arms, burying his face in her hair. She let him. Leaning into him she let the tears flow, washing away her anger until eventually, she was silent. Spent and exhausted.

"I promise nothing happened," Zak whispered.

"I know." She nodded, for deep down, she trusted him, knew he would never betray her in such a way. "I wasn't prepared, that's all. You appeared with her scent on you, her lipstick on you. I reacted."

"I would have done the same if you smelled of another man," he said, rubbing her back.

"I'm sweaty and dirty," she muttered, pulling away from him.

"Better get you cleaned up then." He smirked and she knew where his mind was. In the gutter with hers.

Hand in hand they returned to the house and headed upstairs to the bathroom.

"Bath or shower?" he asked.

"Shower." She stripped while he adjusted the water until the temperature was perfect, then he turned to her. Wrapping a hand around her throat ever so softly he led her back against the tiled wall of the shower, uncaring that he was getting soaked. It wasn't his actions that jump-started her heart, but the raw lust that consumed him. The dark need in his eyes. Her lady bits tingled when his thumb grazed over a hardened nipple, and a jolt of pleasure shot straight to her core.

He covered her mouth with his, his tongue hot as it dived inside her, as he melted her knees and stole her breath. Spinning her, he placed her hands on the wall, then lifted one foot so it rested on the bench in the shower. He wrapped a hand around her throat again and whispered in her ear, "Now I'm going to do things to you," he said, his voice deep and smooth, "very bad things." His words set her soul ablaze. "And you're going to see exactly what it is you do to me." He cupped a breast, kneaded it, grazed his teeth over her lobe, his warm breath fanning her cheek.

He nibbled on her neck, skimmed his fingers over her breasts, fingertips hot against their peaks, causing a spasm of pleasure to shoot through her. His hands brushed over her belly, and her legs started to give way. She laid her head back against his shoulder as his hand reached between her thighs. Holding her to him with one arm, he brushed softly, stroking until the spark he'd ignited blazed to life.

Then he was gone. She opened her eyes to find him on his knees in front of her, his mouth branding her with a fiery kiss. She gasped. Pleasure pulsed through her as his tongue unraveled her. He grazed his teeth along the sensitive apex, then feathered his tongue in sweet, short sweeps, stroking her, coaxing her closer and closer until a riptide of raw lust engulfed her. The orgasm rocked through her, sending out waves of bliss to every nerve in her body. She plunged her fingers into his hair and held him to her as the tidal wave of pleasure washed over her, rocking her to her core.

With the release of all that energy, she almost fell against the tiles, but Zak was behind her at once, his quest only just beginning when he pushed his wet jeans over his hips and entered her from behind in one long thrust. A twinge of delight leaped inside her as the orgasm that had yet to completely fade flared to delighted life.

He pulled her back against him, locking her there as he whispered in her ear, "Come with me again." She focused on him as his powerful strokes fanned the flames. His brows furrowed, his expression one of almost agony as his own climax neared. He braced one hand on the tiles, clenched his jaw. He thrust harder, an exquisite hunger swelling inside her. She felt it the moment he erupted inside her. He groaned as his orgasm crested, as it surged through him and into her. Her lungs seized. Her eyes rolled back as wave after wave of scalding fire crashed into her. The desire was overwhelming and earth shattering and wonderful.

She tumbled to earth slowly and blinked. Disentangling

herself, she turned to him and focused on his impossibly handsome face.

"You undo me. Everything I am is for you. There will never be another. Never." His words thrilled her, growled with an edge of violence as if daring her to disagree. He'd staked his claim. He was hers. She was his. She wouldn't have it any other way.

21

Now that it was time to break the sire bond, something she'd wanted all along, Georgia hesitated. Was it the right thing to do? Was it really that terrible for Zak to have such control over them?

"You're wrong." His words in her ear made her jump. "It's the right thing to do."

"You're sure?" For now, she doubted herself because it was true Zak had never used the bond to his own advantage, had never abused it anyway.

"It's a weakness," he told her now, rubbing his thumb along her lower lip, filling her with warmth. And distracting her from her worries. "I can't afford to be linked to you. Any of you. If I'm killed, I'll be damned if you'll all die with me." His eyes were dark, swirling with not only anger but resolution. He'd sacrifice what he must, do what he must, to keep them all safe.

"I don't want to think about you dying," she muttered, closing her eyes.

"Same goes for me. So do the spell. It'll be fine, we'll all be fine." His mouth dragged over her ear, his teeth tugged at her lobe, and she shivered.

"You're distracting me again," she whispered. A reluctant dimple appeared at the side of his mouth and he stepped back, taking his warmth with him.

"All set?" He glanced at the items she laid out on the top of the bench in their bedroom. Her dagger, candles, a bowl, salt.

"Yeah." With one last long look at him, she tore her eyes away, to the window and the darkness outside. The property was cloaked, a handy spell the witches had sent her way, so Ronan or the demons wouldn't be able to sense, let alone track, her magic. "We need to do this outside."

They gathered in the backyard, barefoot on the lawn. Georgia traced a pentagram pattern on the grass with the salt, placed the candles at each point, then had everyone stand inside, herself included.

"I'm going to need your blood," she told them, holding up the dagger and bowl. Most of the old spells used blood magic.

"I'll go first." Frank maneuvered to stand in front of her, hand held out. She nicked his finger with the dagger, holding the bowl under the small cut and capturing one small drop of blood. Kyan, Cole, and Aston all took turns, then Skye, whose blue eyes were luminous as she looked at Georgia.

"Will there be time for the other?" she whispered, her face pale, shadows beneath her eyes.

"Yes. There's time." After she'd broken the sire bond, she'd invoke Dainton. Capturing the drip of Skye's blood, Georgia nodded at her. Then it was Zak's turn. He remained silent as she sliced the blade over his finger and captured the drop of blood. She couldn't help herself, she raised his hand to her face and kissed the wound, wrapping her lips around the edge of his finger and sucking. His eyes darkened and heat emanated from him.

"Guys," Frank reminded her, "we're all here in rather close quarters."

Smiling, Zak pulled his hand free, took the dagger from her, and pricked her finger so she could capture her own blood. He returned the favor, swiping his tongue along the wound, sealing it. She shivered in the moonlight.

"Okay, here's what's going to happen." She cleared her throat and addressed them all. "I'm going to mix Aurora's blood with ours, then I need to draw a symbol over your heart with the blood. Next, I'll recite the spell and it'll be done. It won't hurt, but don't leave the pentagram until I tell you to, okay?"

Heads nodded and mutters of "got ya" reached her ears with the sounds of shirts being pulled off and tossed on the ground. She made her way around the group, painting an arrow symbol on their skin. Skye pulled aside the strap of her tank, then did the same for Georgia so she could draw the symbol on herself. Finally, they were ready.

"Hold hands," she commanded. Zak clasped her left hand, Skye her right, and they stood in a circle. The moon disappeared behind a cloud, plunging them into temporary darkness.

"Do not let go, do not leave the circle," she reminded them, then closed her eyes, grounded herself, digging her toes into the earth, before she began the spell.

"Frange ad vinculum interpater et vampire. Quad cum esset unus, duas redire. Separatum!" As the last word died on her lips the wind whipped around them, then a bright light shot out from the mark on their chests, joining in the middle of the circle to form a beam straight up into the sky. The light pulsed, then as quickly as it had formed, it disappeared, the wind settled and all was silent.

"It's done," Georgia whispered, releasing Zak and Skye's hands.

"Did it work?" Cole asked.

"Only one way to find out," Zak replied. "Let me see if I can command you." Zak looked at Cole intently, then Aston, Kyan, and Frank. Finally, he looked at Skye, his eyes boring into her. Nothing happened.

"Looks like it may have worked." He grinned.

"What were you trying to order them to do?" Georgia asked suspiciously.

"Kiss each other." Zak chuckled.

The warriors protested. "Hey man, not cool."

"You didn't feel the sudden urge to plant one on each other though, did you?" Zak pointed out.

"No, but geez, dude."

"Can we go now, leave the circle?" Aston asked.

"Sure." Georgia extinguished the candles and stepped outside over the salt boundary.

"What about Dainton?" Skye asked and everyone froze, turning to look at her.

"We'll do that one inside. In your room." Georgia placed her arm around her sister and squeezed. This wasn't going to be easy, on any of them, but if she could give them the chance to say a final farewell then she'd do it.

Linking her arm with Skye, she walked inside, leaving Zak and the warriors to clear up the remnants of the spell. It had worked, they were no longer linked, and thankfully Georgia didn't feel any different. There was no sense of loss. She'd been worried she'd feel it, they all would, like a void, but it was just the same as before.

"Get cleaned up, wash that blood off." She indicated the blood arrow peeking out from the edge of Skye's tank top. "Then I'll meet you in your room. I need to get cleaned up myself and get the candle."

ONCE MORE THE WARRIORS GATHERED, only this time it was in Skye's room.

"*Dainton, audi me, et descenderet. Ambulate in terram usque ad flamma moriatur.*" The candle flickered and then it happened. Dainton appeared.

"What the hell?" he muttered, looking around, confusion stamped across his features.

"Dainton!" Skye cried and rushed to him, but when her hand reached out to touch him it went straight through his shoulder. "Oh!" She gasped, stepping back.

"Remember, he's not corporeal. And you only have until the candle runs out," Georgia reminded her. Dainton turned to look at her, surprise on his face. "Dainton, we've invoked your spirit—I hope you don't mind?" She shrugged a shoulder, a half smile tilting her lips.

"Mind? Of course not! I thought I'd never see you guys again."

"I'm going to say my piece and leave you all to it." Georgia looked at her feet, then back up, directly into Dainton's eyes. "I'm sorry I gave you grief about Skye. I'd been warned you were going to hurt her, break her heart. And you did. But it wasn't by your choosing. So…I'm sorry I got up in your face about that."

"You wouldn't be you if you didn't." Dainton smiled, brought his hand down to rest on her shoulder, only, of course, neither of them could feel it. "But don't rush off on my account. Stay." He waved his arm, indicating the others in the room. "We're all family. And I'm guessing if it weren't for you I wouldn't be standing here now."

Tears filled Georgia's eyes. "Stupid pregnancy hormones," she muttered but leaned gratefully against Zak when he wrapped his arm around her and tugged her into his side.

"And for God's sake, will y'all sit-down or something? You're all standing around gawking at me like I'm some sort of freak. Sit. Chill. Tell me what's been happening. Tell me you've taken down that son of a bitch Ronan."

The warriors chuckled, each finding a comfortable position on the floor, each recounting their stories of the battle still raging with Ronan and brainstorming ways to defeat him. Time passed and when Georgia glanced over at the candle she was shocked, it had burned almost all the way down.

"Guys. It's time to give Dainton and Skye some privacy." She stirred from where she'd almost been dozing, comfortably seated on the floor between Zak's outstretched legs, leaning back against his chest.

Tears clogged her throat at the final goodbyes she witnessed, of her own with the warrior who'd stolen her sister's heart. But with the sadness came a hint of peace. Dainton had told them of the afterlife, how he'd been reunited with his family, his parents and sister who'd died hundreds of years ago, that he was happy and at peace and that he sincerely hoped he didn't see any of them in the afterlife anytime soon.

"Did I make a mistake?" Georgia asked Zak, walking hand in hand with him back to their room.

"What do you mean?"

"Bringing Dainton back. I mean, did you see Skye's face? She was distraught." Guilt ate at her. She'd meant to ease Skye's pain, not increase it.

"You did the right thing. A chance for goodbye, for closure. Sure it's going to hurt. Hell, we're all hurting. But we found out he's in a good place, that's he's with his family. He's happy. Knowing that helps."

She only hoped he was right. She'd never forgive herself if she'd inflicted even more pain on her sister.

22

"It's so obvious I can't believe I didn't think of it before."

"What's that?" Zak stole one of the onion rings from the basket on the table and she slapped his hand away. Frank was catering to her latest craving—she didn't know what she'd do without his culinary skills, starve most likely.

"I know how to find Ronan." She shoved an onion ring into her mouth, knowing she'd pay for it with heartburn later but unable to resist the tasty morsels. How she hadn't doubled her own body weight by now she didn't know, but she'd retained her physique despite her pregnant belly that sat out in front like she'd shoved a basketball under her shirt.

"Oh? How?" Everyone looked at her and she held out her wrist.

"Ronan's mark. He's connected to me, right? We're assuming he can track me through this, so then it only makes sense that I can track him too."

Zak clasped her hand across the table, rubbing his thumb over the ugly black mark.

"Is it dangerous?" he asked.

"I'll just use a locator spell, that's easy enough. I didn't think to use it before because we needed something of Ronan's to make it work. Now I have something of his, the essence of his magic. The spell will work for sure. The thing is, I'll have to assume he'll feel it or sense it in some way. So we won't have the element of surprise."

"I've got an idea on that," Rhys piped up. "Rather than us going to him, we wait. Let him come to us. His ego would demand it, don't you think? If he feels you're doing the spell he won't be able to sit tight. In fact, he'd probably be very surprised that you're well enough to do any spells—he'd be assuming you're on death's door considering his mark is poisoning you."

"I like that idea." Zak nodded. "We can choose a location away from humans, away from our home."

"Why not the first warehouse in Redmeadows?" Georgia suggested. "It has a poetic sense of justice about it."

"So we lure him to the warehouse with your locator spell. Then what?" Rhys asked.

"We need Marcus." Pulling out her phone, Georgia dialed the angel's number.

"You rang?" Marcus appeared by the side of their table, grinning, a bottle of whiskey in one hand, glass in the other.

"Did you come from the pub?"

"But of course. So judgy," he whined, dropping into an empty chair. He filled his glass and took a gulp.

She'd seen him down glass after glass of straight whiskey now, yet he didn't appear remotely drunk. Were angels immune to alcohol?

"If only darlin'," he interrupted her thoughts, winking at her. "We just need a whole lot more than mere mortals for it to have any effect. And even then the buzz doesn't last long."

"You read my mind?" Oh no, not another mind-reading angel. It was bad enough Zak had the ability, although she couldn't really complain since he couldn't actually read her, only if he drank her blood.

Marcus shook his head. "Your face. You're very expressive."

"Tell Zak what you told us. About his magic."

"Straight to the point." Marcus laughed. "I like you."

Zak growled, shifting slightly in his chair to glare at the other angel. "Take it easy, bro."

Marcus laughed even harder. "Oh, this is priceless."

"What's so funny?" Zak demanded, anger emanating from him in waves.

"You are. Settle down, big fella, you two are fated mates. C'mon, you know this already. Don't get all twitchy because I'm talking to her. You're as bad as the wolves."

"What?" Now it was Rhys's turn, his hackles rising.

"Cut it out, Marcus," Georgia scolded. "You're a trouble-maker, I see. But we have a common goal—or should I say, enemy—here and you said you wanted in. If that's still the case, pull your head in."

"Oh, I do love alpha women." Marcus sighed. "Okay, okay, I'll behave. So Zachariah my man, you think if you use your magic you'll lose control and destroy the planet?"

Zak nodded, for once speechless.

"That is, as they say, a load of hogwash. What better way to get someone to stop using magic than to make them afraid of it." He refilled his whiskey glass again, took a hefty gulp, and eyed Zak over the rim of his glass.

"I can see the cogs turning," he told Georgia, waiting as Zak processed what he'd said.

"You're saying that someone—Ronan—messed with my head and made me believe my magic was dangerous."

"Correct." Marcus nodded, busy refilling his glass. Georgia clasped Zak's hand, bringing his attention back to her.

"It makes sense. Ronan messed with your head once. We thought we'd sorted through all that, but what if there's more? What if your magic isn't dangerous at all?"

"We don't have time to do another meditation." Zak frowned.

"So we take a chance." She squeezed his hand.

"It's risky."

"What's risky is doing nothing and letting Ronan friggin win," Marcus muttered into his glass.

"Why mark me though? Why drag me into it if he's beef is with his brother?" Georgia frowned, rubbing at her wrist.

"My best guess? He's been unable to get hold of Zak, then when he finally finds him, it's too late, the prophecy is in motion. So he has to change his plans, modify them. He tried to stop you from becoming a witch, yes? Sent the Hunter after you. Didn't work, you not only defeated the Hunter but you inherited all of the magic the Hunter had collected. I bet Ronan hadn't been expecting that. All of a sudden you're his golden egg. Your magic could be all he needs to fuel his Nephilim army. He just needs to get it out of you. And in the meantime, he can harvest the witches while he tries to get his hands on you. Maybe the witches' magic would have been enough to lay a trap for you. In a way it worked, he managed to mark you."

"It does make sense. And you're going to have to cut back on those if you want to help," Georgia told him, nodding toward the glass he'd raised to his lips. He frowned at her, then nodded. Waving his hand, the bottle and glass disappeared.

"I'll be sober in an hour," he told her, then slapped a hand on Zak's shoulder. "So, we doing this?"

Shaking his head, Zak sighed. "Yeah, I guess we are."

Zak and Marcus gathered the warriors. The plan was

they'd teleport to the warehouse in Redmeadows. Rhys and Georgia were going by car.

"I just need to pee," she told Rhys as she pushed out of her chair.

"Want food for the drive?" Rhys asked, already pulling open the fridge and peering inside.

"You're such a good friend." Georgia grinned, calling over her shoulder, "And yes, I could really go for some of that chocolate cake Frank baked earlier."

"I can't believe how much you friggin eat." Shaking his head, Rhys pulled out the cake. He debated cutting her a slice then decided to bring the whole thing. He was pretty sure she'd eat it all before the night was out.

"Did you bring the map?"

"Here." Zak unfolded the map and smoothed it out on the floor of the warehouse.

"Help me down," Georgia said, holding out her hands. Zak slipped an arm around her shoulders and helped her kneel in front of the map. Taking the dagger in her hand, Georgia glanced at the warriors gathered around her.

"Are you ready?" she asked. They nodded, faces solemn. Everyone here tonight had revenge on their minds. Ronan would pay for killing Dainton; they wouldn't let him escape again. Marcus was over in the shadows leaning against the wall and watching with passive disinterest. She hadn't been able to work him out, not really. She was pretty sure the drunken jokester persona he presented was false, hiding a pain that ate away at him inside, but she didn't know the angel well enough to get him to confide in her. She just hoped the trust they'd put in him wasn't misplaced.

Holding out her arm, she sliced across Ronan's mark with

the dagger, wincing at the sting. Blood tinged a little too black dripped onto the map.

"*Quid quaeris, ex dominus signum, invenietis est magicae,*" she chanted. Placing her palm over her bleeding arm she whispered, "*Sana,*" and the wound healed.

They watched as the blood drops moved around the map, haphazard at first before coming together in one place. Kanurbury.

"It worked." She smiled, holding out her hand so Zak could help her to her feet.

"Now we need to get you to safety." Keeping a hold of her hand, he led her across the warehouse to the pentagram she'd drawn earlier with salt. She snapped her fingers and the candles at each of the points flared, flames flickering. Marcus had given her a powder to mix with the salt, a compound that would stop the Nephilim from touching her. Once she stepped across the boundary and into the center of the pentagram she'd be safe. Untouchable.

She stepped inside just in time. The warehouse was suddenly overrun with close to a hundred demons. Facing them she held out her hands. "*Metuendas Dcemonis violentias, ab hoc imperium sempiternum. Relinquo,*" she shouted. Her magic shot out across the warehouse in an invisible wave, the demons instantly vanishing.

"Impressive little witch. I'm surprised you're still standing." Ronan mocked her from the shadows at the far end of the warehouse. Surrounding him were twenty or more Nephilim, effectively blocking him from view.

Zak, Marcus, and the warriors sprang into action, engaging the Nephilim in battle. Swords rang out, the clash loud and echoing all around her while Georgia looked on, safe in her pentagram. Or so she thought. Suddenly Ronan was in front of her, an evil grin on his face.

"You think you're so clever," he taunted, "but you forget

you bear my mark. I can do *this* and you're screwed." He twisted his hand and pain shot through her arm. Pulling up her sleeve she saw the black veins spreading, fast. Before her horrified eyes they reached her elbow, then her shoulder.

"No," she gasped, dropping to her knees and closing her eyes, trying to force the dark magic back, to stop it from spreading.

"Fight it!" Marcus spear tackled Ronan, sending them both crashing into the far wall.

Georgia clutched at her chest. It was hard to breathe, she couldn't get enough oxygen, and she felt strange and sluggish. He was winning. Ronan's mark was killing her. And Jelly Bean. Tears slid down her cheeks as she curled into a ball, hugging her baby bump. Then the pain started, burning like fire through her veins. She screamed, her body stretching taut. She was dimly aware she'd kicked a candle over, that the scrape of her foot had most likely broken the barrier of her pentagram, but it didn't matter. She was dying anyway. Any second. The burning in her veins was intense, but slowing, as was her heartbeat.

"Sorry." She sobbed, clutching her belly. "I'm sorry I couldn't save you, baby."

She felt Jelly Bean kick, knew it would be the last time she'd feel her move, that she'd never get to hold her in her arms. A wail tore from her throat. This was so unfair. They'd come so far, it couldn't end like this. And then something happened. She felt the dark magic retreating; her heartbeat settled back into its normal rhythm. Had Ronan been killed?

Struggling to sit up, she looked around, caught sight of Ronan in the midst of battle, still alive. As the dark magic receded she could feel it on her skin, at her shoulder and move down her arm, back to her wrist where it originated. She watched, mesmerized, as a white glow banded her arm and pushed the dark magic out. At Ronan's mark, the white glow stopped and pulsed. Then with an audible pop, the magic disappeared. And so did Ronan's mark.

"Was...was that you, Jelly Bean?" she whispered in wonder, pressing a hand to the side of her belly. A distinct kick against her palm was her answer. "Oh, you beautiful, amazing, wonderful baby," she cooed. "Thank you." The sounds of fighting intruded, reminding her she was a sitting duck with the ward of the pentagram broken.

"Let's get this fixed." On her knees she leaned over and smoothed out the scattered salt and powder, repairing the break in the seal. She was about to relight the candle when it happened. She didn't see him coming, had no idea he was upon her until an arm banded around her chest and pulled her backward. She heard Zak scream her name and then nothing.

23

"**Y**ou asshole." Georgia spat, tugging at the metal restraints pinning her to what was, for all intents and purposes, an altar. "You teleported me. You could have hurt my baby!"

Ronan laughed, tossing her dagger over and over in his hands. "That's the least of your worries, Witch. You removed my mark. How?"

"How do you think?" She jerked at her wrists again, the metal cutting into her skin.

"I think it was your unborn baby here." He rested the blade of the dagger across her swollen abdomen and she froze, not daring to breathe. Where the hell was Zak? And Marcus?

"Oh?" She bluffed, trying to buy time. Ronan laughed, removing the dagger, he walked around the altar she lay on.

"Don't play innocent. We all know this baby is powerful, perhaps the most powerful being on earth—should it be born." Georgia shuddered at his words. He was going to kill her baby. She tugged at her restraints again. Why couldn't she budge them? Were they warded in some way? She sent a message to Jelly Bean, asking for help, but none was forth-coming. Was she asleep?

"Now that I have you exactly where I want you I really don't have time to waste." Ronan stepped into her line of vision, a helmet similar to what they'd found in the ware-house dangling from his fingers. Twisting her head she looked behind her to see a smaller version of the machine he'd used to steal the witches' magic. "It'd be nice to chat and let you in on all my plans, but alas, that brother of mine is never far away. To be honest I'm amazed he's managed to piece it together so far. I thought I'd wiped everything from his mind, but it seems not. Perhaps you had something to do with that, hmm?" He was by her side now, level with her hips and she gulped when she saw the murderous gleam in his eyes.

"Please don't hurt my baby." She whispered in horror, trying to jerk her head away when he clamped the helmet over her skull.

"Here's the thing." He pulled the straps tight beneath her chin, "to siphon your baby's magic…I need it out of your belly. Since I don't have time to wait around for you to go into labor, I'm going to have to speed things along." He'd bent and picked something up; when she squinted, he held it up higher so she could see. Her dagger. Oh shit, he had her dagger.

"Wait!" She gasped, watching in horror as he pushed her top up with one hand, getting ready to slice open her belly with the other.

"I've waited too long as it is. You'll probably die. Bleed out. But I can steal your magic while that happens." The dagger flew down and she screamed, screwing her eyes shut and waiting for the pain. When it didn't come she cracked open an eye. The dagger was suspended above her belly, Ronan trying to force it to pierce her flesh, but it was as if she had a force field around her. Jelly Bean. She smiled.

"Get away from her!" Zak roared. His eyes glowing green, he threw out his hand and a beam of green light shot out, propelling Ronan away from her. She heard him crash into the wall behind her head.

Ronan laughed. "Finally clued in, brother?" He sent his own bolt of magic hurtling at Zak, propelling him away from Georgia. Turning her head she watched as Ronan pulled himself to his feet, one arm pulled back as if to throw a base-ball, instead, he threw magic. Zak braced himself and raised both hands, palms facing Ronan. His magic met Ronan's head-on, clashing where they met, irresistible force against irresistible force. Both men deflected at once, magic crashing to the side, ripping holes in the walls.

"Hey there, sugar," Marcus murmured by her ear, "you going to lie there all day or should we get out of here?" He winked, snapping his fingers and releasing her from her bonds. The helmet fell to the floor with a clatter.

"Incoming," he muttered, pulling her off the slab of concrete that served as an altar and tucking her down beside it, leaning over her to protect her from the debris currently flying around the room.

"We can't leave him," Georgia protested, pushing his arm aside to peek over the altar. It appeared as if Ronan and Zak were taking it in turns to throw each other around the room. She could see Zak's flashes of magic, tinted with green, while Ronan's were dark.

"Your man can take care of himself, believe me." Marcus pushed her head down. "But if you get clocked in the head by a chunk of concrete I'm not taking the blame, so keep your bloody head down."

The earth shuddered beneath their feet and Georgia grimaced. She wasn't sure where they were but it didn't feel safe. If the two of them kept ripping holes in the walls and roof the whole structure was going to collapse around them. She popped up for another peek, ignoring Marcus's exasperated sigh.

"Why aren't you helping?" she accused, frowning when she noticed Zak appeared to be tiring. He wasn't accustomed to using magic. That he had done so effectively up until now was a testament to him, but now his blows were going wide, weakening in their intensity. She needed to distract Ronan, give Zak time to refocus, to call on his inner strength. Peering around the room, she realized they were on a stage, and beyond was what appeared to be an old theater. Judging by the condition of the place, no performances had taken place here for many years, which meant they were most likely in Kanurbury, the capital of deserted buildings.

Spying the faded stage curtains she clicked her fingers and flames began to lick at the bottom, soon taking hold and soaring up the rotting fabric.

"I'm not sure that was wise," Marcus muttered in her ear. "We don't need to be toasted."

"Shhh, it'll be fine." Her plan had worked, up to a point. The flames got Ronan's attention, but also Zak's. Shit, he needed to focus, to rebuild his magic. Or failing that, get a weapon. Just as the thought entered her mind her eyes landed on her dagger lying on the floor a few feet away. Narrowing her eyes she sent the dagger sliding across the floor to hit Zak in the boot with a flick of her finger.

Glancing down, Zak's eyebrows shot into his hairline with surprise. He glanced up, saw her hovering behind the altar and cocked his head to the side.

"Use the dagger," she whispered. Inside she could feel her own magic swirling and tumbling, she could hear the witches whose magic now resided in her, chanting "use the dagger, use the dagger."

Zak bent and picked up the dagger. He tested the weight of it in his palm, fingers wrapping around the handle. That's when it happened. The dagger glowed, the familiar green of Zak's magic.

"Heads up, buddy," Marcus called out. Both Zak and Georgia had been so enthralled with the dagger that they hadn't noticed Ronan's attention move from the fire back to Zak. Now a blast of magic hit him in the shoulder, sending him in a cartwheel backward. Without releasing his grasp on the dagger Zak righted himself and, dagger in one hand, a force field of magic in the other, he leaped at Ronan, slashing with the dagger.

The front of Ronan's shirt tore and blood seeped through, yet no wound could be seen. What was this? Zak didn't slow down to wonder. He came at Ronan, inflicting slice after slice, blood appearing on his clothing but still no wounds. Whatever the reason, it was enough to destroy Ronan's concentration, his magic now useless. He must've known it too, for he bent and picked up a two by four from the ground and swung. Zak ducked, then pounced, sinking the blade into Ronan's stomach. Before he could push the blade up and into the angel's heart, Ronan ground his thumbs into Zak's eyes. Hard.

Cursing, Zak rolled away, temporarily blinded. On hands and knees, he shook his head, waiting for his vision to clear. Ronan rolled to his stomach and tried to crawl away, but he was severely injured, and with his magic depleted, his ability to heal himself was less than efficient. Both men stopped, panting, and eyed each other.

"Never thought you had it in you, brother," Ronan wheezed.

"Never thought I'd have to kill my own flesh and blood," Zak shot back, voice cold.

"You don't have to. We can come to an agreement."

"Doubtful."

"Don't believe a word that lying piece of shit says," Marcus called out. Ronan swiveled is head in surprise.

"Marcus? Is that you? What are you doing here, buddy? Come to help a mate out?"

Marcus rose to his feet, stretching his wings behind him.

"I've come for retribution." He stalked toward Ronan who wriggled back until he was pressed up against a wall, hand to his bleeding stomach, invisible slashes on his arms still dripping blood.

"You killed her, and for that, you will die." Marcus's voice dripped ice and Georgia shivered. She'd never heard him speak like this before.

"Who? Come on, Marcus, you know you have to be specific." Ronan sighed wearily, his arrogant tone making him seem oblivious to the danger he was in.

"My *wife*," Marcus spat, face contorted with anger and pain. "You killed my wife and my unborn child, you piece of shit!"

Georgia gasped, hands clutching her belly. How awful. No wonder Marcus hated Ronan.

"You knew there were risks," Ronan replied.

"You promised they wouldn't be involved. That if I did what you wanted, they would be left out of it. Yet you killed them anyway. Just for the fun of it."

"Oh come on, Marcus, not for fun." Ronan sneered. "Oh okay, it was a little bit fun. I needed to keep you in line. You wanted out and I couldn't have that. What better way to control you than to take away what you love the most."

"Stupid mistake," Marcus spat. "The best way to control me would have been to keep them alive. Because without them, I am nothing. I don't care what happens to me. The only thing I want in this life…is to see you dead." He flapped his wings and moved closer, a sword appearing in his hand.

"Hey now!" Ronan finally cottoned on that he was in real trouble, panic flashing over his face. An angel's sword was deadly, especially to another angel. He glanced at Zak who stood at the ready, the dagger in his hand, and the approaching angel with his wings spanning almost the entire width of the stage, a sword glowing white in his hand. Holy retribution.

Georgia sucked in a breath and held it, watching as Marcus stood over Ronan, feet planted on either side, the tip of his sword resting above Ronan's heart.

"Any last words?"

"Don't be hasty!" Ronan shouted, sweat beading his skin. "Let's talk about this. I'm sorry. I'm sorry I killed them. I can bring them back, with my magic and hers"—he pointed to Georgia—"we'd have the power we needed."

"You can't bring back the dead," Georgia cut in. "That's dark magic and there's a balance, a price must always be paid. If you bring back the dead, one you love must die in their place."

Marcus inclined his head slightly in her direction, understanding her intentions. She didn't want him to be swayed by Ronan's bargaining skills.

"She's been dead a hundred years, moron. There's no coming back." Idly he trailed the sword over Ronan's chest, then arm. Near his elbow he pressed, the blade cutting into the flesh as Marcus mimicked the scar on his own arm.

"Hurts like a bitch, doesn't it?" He raised a brow, resting the sword once more on Ronan's chest. "Ever wonder what it felt like to have your heart cut right out of your chest?" Marcus's voice had lost its icy edge, now he was back to the cocky and brash angel Georgia knew. He cocked his head, waiting for Ronan's response. When none was forthcoming he prodded him with the sword. "No?"

Ronan grunted. "No."

"Well, physically speaking, neither do I." Marcus shrugged. "But metaphorically? Metaphorically you ripped my heart out the day they died. But I'm not here to talk about my pain, I'm here for yours." He twisted to look over his shoulder. "Zak, my man, I crashed your party. You want in on this?"

"He's all yours. You deserve it more than me," Zak told him, although he didn't relax his stance one iota. Ronan was wily. They couldn't let their guard down and risk him escaping.

"I think we're equal. He killed your folks and fucked with your head. Tried to take your woman and child." His eyes flared at the reminder of all he lost.

"He's all yours," Zak assured him.

"What are you waiting for?" Ronan goaded. "Too scared? Can't follow through?"

"Just enjoying the moment. But you're right. Time to move things along. I'm sick of hearing your voice and I know no matter what drivel may fall from your mouth while you beg for your life, you don't mean any of it. I'd say rest in peace, but you don't deserve it. May you burn in hell." With that Marcus thrust the sword through Ronan's chest. Ronan gasped, then gurgled, his face registering his surprise. Had he thought Marcus wouldn't go through with it? Did he think he was going to walk away, unpunished for what he'd done?

Blood bubbled out of his mouth and he tried to draw a breath, but there's no coming back from a sword through your heart. His head flopped forward, blood dribbling from his mouth down to mingle with the stain spreading across his chest.

With a satisfied nod, Marcus withdrew his sword, cleaned the blade on Ronan's pant leg, then swung it over his shoulder to nestle it among his wings, which retracted and disappeared.

"Well, hasn't this been an exciting day." Marcus turned, eyeing them both and rubbing his palms together. "What's next?"

"I think we've had enough excitement for one day," Zak muttered, relaxing his stance, the green glow fading from his eyes.

"There is one other thing." Georgia moved out from behind the altar. She indicated her wet pants and soaked shoes. "My water broke."

"Oh shit!" Zak exclaimed, rushing to her.

"Exactly." She grinned, then winced as a contraction rippled across her abdomen.

THEY SAY you don't remember the pain of giving birth. That's not true. Georgia remembered plenty. Zak's panic at getting her home. Rhys calling in his pack doctor to help with the birth, Skye holding her hand and telling her to breathe. Zak kneeling behind her on the bed, supporting her, telling her he loved her constantly, so much so that she threatened to squeeze his nuts instead of his hand if he didn't shut up. The warriors, pacing around downstairs, anxious for news.

Ten hours. Ten excruciating hours filled with tears, tantrums and finally acceptance. Now, as she looked into the eyes of her daughter, Georgia knew every second had been worth it.

"She's beautiful," Zak whispered, tears in his eyes as he looked down at the pink bundle clasped to Georgia's chest.

"She is perfect," Georgia replied, serene and filled with so much love she thought her heart might explode from it. "Hey, Jelly Bean." She rested her lips upon her baby's forehead and sent a prayer to her parents who she hoped were watching. She'd done it. She was a mom.

"We can't keep calling her Jelly Bean," Zak protested, settling himself behind her on their bed and pulling her to rest against his chest, the baby in her arms.

"Jade Brielle," Georgia announced.

Zak squeezed her. "Brielle? After my mother? How did you know?"

Georgia shrugged. "I just did. And her initials stay the same. JB for Jelly Bean and JB for Jade Brielle."

"It's perfect. Everything is perfect."

"There. Take a look." Georgia opened her eyes. Sheena held a mirror in front of her and Georgia looked into it. She looked...beautiful.

"Oh my god," she breathed.

"Hold still. I'm almost finished with your hair," Lisa muttered from behind her, a bobby pin gripped between her teeth.

"You guys are amazing. Thank you so much for this."

"Oh my God, I can't believe you're finally doing it!" Skye zipped around the room, a hyperactive ball of energy. Georgia smiled at her. Skye's grief over Dainton had been all encompassing. They'd gotten their final goodbyes, but that was just the thing, wasn't it? They were final. Skye had pulled away from warrior duty, as Georgia called it, and had been spending more and more time at their antique store. She was even talking about moving back into the apartment upstairs.

"Skye! Please. Take it down a notch or three or you're going to make me really, really nervous."

"Sorry. Here. Champagne!" She pressed a flute into her sister's hand.

Georgia turned away from her reflection in the mirror. Her white gown hung in the window, waiting for her to slip it on.

"You look beautiful." Skye stood looking at her, her eyes shining.

"Don't you dare cry. You'll make me cry and ruin my makeup," Georgia scolded, taking a hefty gulp of champagne.

Outside she could hear sounds of activity. Crossing to the window she peered out. Preparations for the wedding were in full swing: the arch covered with roses in place, row upon row of wooden chairs, decorated with vines, in place in the garden.

Holding the ceremony at the farmhouse had been Zak's idea, and he and the warriors had taken care of everything, transforming the garden into a magical fairyland. In the trees hung twinkling fairy lights. The barn had been opened up and housed the bar and trestles laden with food, out front a dance floor. Georgia smiled. It was perfect. Today would be perfect.

"Someone wanted her momma," Frank said from the doorway.

"JB!" Georgia smiled, her heart full to bursting. Today their family would be complete. Whole. She'd never felt happier and needed to pinch herself to make sure this was real. JB squealed and wriggled when she clapped eyes on Georgia, holding her arms out demanding to be handed over. With a chuckle, Frank handed the baby over.

"Five minutes, Miss," he told her, rubbing the back of his knuckles on her rosy cheek. "Your mom and dad have a wedding to get to. And you need to get changed into your pretty dress."

"Hello, my darling girl." Georgia pressed her lips to JB's forehead, smiling when she left a lipstick imprint. "Have you been good for Uncle Frank?" JB answered in her own nonsensical baby language, gurgling and dribbling with apparent joy. Her chubby little arms waved and the flowers in the vase by the bed levitated, circling their heads.

"Okay, young lady, enough of that." Georgia laughed, waving her hand to return the flowers to the vase.

"Guests are starting to arrive!" Aston called from downstairs.

Chest suddenly constricting, it hit Georgia. She was doing this. Marrying the man of her dreams. Today. Skye scooped JB from her arms, nuzzling her niece and making her squeal with delight before depositing her back in Frank's arms and shooing him from the room.

"Time for the bride to get dressed," Skye declared, closing the door lest someone else decided to pop up for a visit. Taking the dress from where it hung over the curtain rail, Skye removed the coat hanger and held it out to Georgia.

"I'm really doing this." Georgia breathed, shrugging out of her silk robe and tossing it on the bed, allowing Skye, Lisa, and Sheena to help her into her dress. It was a simple white sheath, hugging her curves before flaring out at her knees. The fabric had a delicate embossed floral pattern and it was divine.

"Oh, Georgia. You're so beautiful. The dress is amazing. It's gorgeous, so graceful and elegant."

Lisa stepped behind to fasten the row of pearl buttons, then fixed the veil in her hair on the antique comb that had belonged to Georgia's grandmother. Sheena stepped forward to retouch the soft rose of her lipstick, then all three women stood looking at her with tears in their eyes.

"If you lot don't cut it out you're going to make me cry and all this will have been for nothing!" Georgia scolded. Never in her life had she felt so pampered, feminine and beautiful. "Thank you for being here today, for being my bridesmaids."

"We wouldn't have it any other way." Skye hugged her, looking stunning herself in her pale blue dress.

"You don't think I've gone too mad, do you?" Georgia chewed on a nail, worry on her face.

"What do you mean?"

"Well, everyone will be expecting a traditional wedding and this is...not."

"It's not about anyone else," Lisa scolded. "This is your day. Yours and Zak's. It doesn't matter what anyone else wants or thinks, but just so you know, I think it's going to be perfect."

It was true. With only Skye as family, she had no one to walk her down the aisle, so she had vetoed the whole idea, deciding to walk herself down the aisle. And instead of flowers, her bridesmaids would precede her with tea light candles inside locus-shaped holders cupped in their hands.

"It's plenty traditional," Sheena argued. "You've got a white dress and veil, you've got a wedding arch, a smoking hot groom and you're saying vows. What more do you need?"

Georgia laughed. What more indeed. It had been six months since Ronan was defeated and JB—Jade Brielle—was born. Lying in Zak's arms after the birth of their daughter, she'd let him pin her down on a wedding date. The cheeky bastard had gotten her at a weak moment, but in all honesty, she couldn't be happier.

Before leaving town Marcus had dug up the final piece to the puzzle. Ronan had found Zak in Eden Hills due to Veronica. He'd stumbled upon her quite by accident and had felt his brother's energy on her. He'd befriended the vampire, gotten into her head, and convinced her to betray Zak. It was the one piece of the puzzle Georgia had never been able to figure out: why Veronica had turned on them. But now it made sense. She'd been tricked and used, just like Ronan had tricked and used many before her. He'd fed her the information about the ancient vampire Marius, how to awaken him and why doing so seemed like a good idea.

He was the one who'd spelled the Hunter and sentenced him to a life of misery. All because of his desire for power, to rule the Earth, his own ego so huge he could never see that eventually the way he treated others would come back to haunt him. Or in this case, stab him in the heart.

"It's almost time." Skye clasped her hand.

"One last peek," Georgia begged, dragging Skye over to the window, watching as guests got out of their cars. Erik from the pub, their employees from the store, a few of the police officers she'd had dealings with over the years, the witches they'd rescued. Rhys showed up next, looking delicious in a charcoal suit and tie. Members of his pack turned up, looking mighty fine in their Sunday best, plus many vampires Georgia hadn't met before but Zak had had dealings with over the years. Even Zak's publisher was here.

There was Aston, talking earnestly with Cole, straightening the white wooden chairs on the lawn. Kyan had stolen JB away from Frank, who was supervising the buffet. Then Marcus, surrounded by a flurry of women, his dimpled smile charming them.

"Ready?" Skye whispered, brushing her knuckles across Georgia's cheek. Nerves made Georgia's stomach clench. She looked down at herself then back at her sister.

"Do you think Zak will like it?"

"Please." She laughed. "Zak is going to trip over his own tongue when he sees you."

Skye waved her forward, with Lisa and Sheena rushing ahead and down the stairs. The girls each wore a dress in a different pastel color, swirls of chiffon dancing around their legs—they looked like they'd stepped out of the pages of a fairy tale.

Skye peeked out the back door and signaled Frank. The sounds of conversation muted, the guests took their seats, and Georgia's heart raced. The music started. The girls picked up their candles and Georgia lit them with a snap of her fingers. In her hands, she held a bouquet of wild flowers. With a deep breath, Lisa went down the aisle first. As her foot hit the carpet, rose petals fell from the sky, softly raining down.

Georgia caught a glimpse of JB who'd spied the petals and was trying to catch them. In her excitement magic was leaking out, sending small sparkles like fireworks into the sky. Zak was going to have to compel their human guests to forget the unexplainable effects they'd witness today. She grinned.

Then it was Sheena's turn, then Skye. Before she left, Skye turned, forcing herself not to cry. She leaned in and gave Georgia one more colossal hug as a tear escaped despite her best efforts. Then it was Georgia's turn. Staring straight ahead, concentrating on her breathing, she stepped forward. Heads turned, she could feel them watching her, but she only had eyes for one. Zak, standing there in a black tux, white shirt, and black bow tie. He looked just as sexy in a tux as he did in a T-shirt and jeans. His wide shoulders. His handsome face, with its strong jaw and sculpted mouth. His thick dark lashes framing his mesmerizing eyes. It didn't matter what he wore because it was Zak himself who stole her breath.

One corner of his mouth tipped up as he watched her. She had to stop herself from sprinting into his arms. Instead, she focused on the music, on keeping time, one foot after the other, her cheeks burning. She could hear the snap of cameras and the whisper of words of praise, but her attention stayed on Zak.

When she reached the front, the minister raised his hands and gestured for everyone to sit.

"Who gives this woman to be married to this man?" he asked.

"I, her sister, Skye Pearce." Skye's voice quivered ever so slightly. She turned to Georgia, her blue eyes shimmering. She gave her a quick hug, then took Georgia's hand and placed it gently into Zak's, holding Georgia's bouquet of flowers.

With both of her hands clasped tightly in his, Georgia raised her eyes to Zak, lost again in his gaze.

"Most of my life," Zak began, his eyes never leaving her, "I've taken each day as it comes, believing that things just happen without any sort of rhyme or reason. And then I met you. And that's when I began believing in destiny and meant to be's, of stars aligned when fate brought me to your door.

"That's when the first spark made me burn for you because you've shown me that there is good in this world. Georgia, you are such a gifted and strong woman, you've been my teacher, my confidant, my lover and best friend. You showed me a ferocious love that I didn't know could exist.

"I see perfection in your eyes, I feel perfection on your skin, I taste perfection on your lips, I hear perfection every time you say I love you. And together we created perfection —our daughter.

"And me, being a man, I'm more accustomed to being flawed, but somehow you've still chosen to give me your love. So I tell you now that these words that I say are not just words; they're my attempt to convey to you, that without you —I'm nothing. It doesn't matter where I go or what I do, you will always be with me.

"I'm going to love you with every fiber of my being; I'm going to love you with a passion that'll bring the world to its knees. I'm going to wage war with your demons so you can rest your head at night. I'm going to tuck your hair behind your ear and press my lips to yours because you just need to be kissed. I'm going to remind you every day how you completely unravel me because your touch upon my skin always has and always will light the darkest parts of my soul.

"So today I ask you to remember one thing. That these words are not just words. They're my vow to you. That I will never leave you. That I will never stop loving you. That there will never be a day that you have to face without me, because you, my sweet beautiful girl, are my life, my love, my only, and I love you."

Georgia blinked, her eyes filled with tears. Zak's vows touched her very soul. Smiling softly, he released her hands to wipe her tears away, before taking her hands in his once more.

Now it was her turn.

"Two years ago you moved to this city. I'll never forget the moment we first met. In person." His brow quirked at her clarification, a subtle dig at their very first meeting, in her dreams. "The spark that was immediately apparent. Although I, being stubborn as usual, refused to believe it."

Their guests chuckled and Zak squeezed her hands.

"I looked into your eyes and I knew, I just knew that I'd found something so profound, it was almost familiar. From so early on you became a huge part of my life, my dreams, my future, and my family. The love that we share cannot possibly be defined by the words that we say today. That is why standing here today I can tell you without any uncertainty that I did, I do, and I always will, choose you. With you, I have found my place in this world. I feel safe with you. Everything in me recognizes you as my home. I love you. You're my man. For always."

The minister went through the rest of the ceremony quickly, and Georgia couldn't recall who said what or what had really happened beyond their vows to each other. She couldn't take her eyes off her handsome new husband. When

Zak slid a hand around the back of her neck and tilted her face to his, she was dazed. When his mouth came down on hers and the crowd cheered, her legs wobbled. It was over. They were married. After all the preparation and work, the planning, anxiety, it was done.

"Look at me."

She opened her dazed eyes and stared into the depths of his. Heat swirled, and desire licked at her skin.

"Doing okay?" he murmured a dark brow arching. She nodded. Yes. More than okay, she was perfect. This day was perfect.

He smiled. "I don't think I've ever seen you this quiet." He nuzzled her cheek, arms sliding around her waist to pull her against him.

"I'm a little overwhelmed," she whispered in return, vaguely aware that they were still standing under the arch and their guests were still watching avidly.

"No regrets?"

She heard the doubt in his voice and cupped his face between her palms. "Nope. Not a single one. I've never been happier, husband." She grinned and she felt the relief flood through him.

"Come on then, wife, let's get this party started." Taking her hand in his, he walked her back down the aisle to the cheers of their guests. Frank stood at the end with JB on his hip. She immediately reached out for Georgia when they grew near and Georgia scooped up her daughter, nestling her between them, smiling adoringly at Zak over her head.

"We did it."

"We certainly did." Leaning over, he pressed his lips to hers, whispering to her, "I have everything I ever wanted. A wife. A family. I couldn't be happier or more proud of my beautiful bride."

Her mouth opened beneath his, her lips welcoming him.

"I wish we were alone," he growled, kissing along her jaw. She laughed, tilting her head back.

"We have plenty of time."

"A lifetime of forever's," he murmured.

"That sounds perfect."

Arms around each other, their daughter in the middle of their embrace, so began the beginning of their forever.

The End

If you like fast-paced paranormal romantic suspense, thrilling heroes, and sassy, kick-ass heroines then swing on by my website for a free book!
http://janehinchey.com/free-book/

NOTES FROM THE AUTHOR

Wow. Here we are at the end of the Awakening Series. What a ride!

If you've followed the series from book one, First Blade, you'll know I originally wrote that story as a stand alone. It wasn't until my readers kept asking me to continue the story for Georgia and Zak that I entertained the idea for a series, and now I feel their story is complete. Don't worry though, I have a couple of spin-off books in the works, Rhys's story, Immortal Ties is coming soon, and I have a little something in mind for Skye.

I've also been asked multiple times if we'll hear anymore from JB. My motto is 'never say never,' so although I have no immediate plans for JB I'm sure her voice will pop up at some point demanding to be heard - and as most writers will tell you, once the voices start you have no choice but to listen!

In the meantime, I'm working on a brand new series, Hell's Gate, where you'll get to meet Lucifer in all her glory. Make sure you swing on by my website to check it out.

If you enjoyed First Blood, please consider leaving a positive review or rating on the site where you purchased it. Reader reviews help my books continue to be valued by resellers and help new readers make decisions about reading them.

You are the reason I write these stories and I sincerely appreciate each of you!

Many thanks for your support!

~ *Jane Hinchey*

ABOUT THE AUTHOR

Aussie Author, Jane Hinchey writes sexy, snarky, badass, paranormal romance and suspense.

Living in the City of Churches (aka Adelaide, South Australia) with her man, two cats, and turtle, she spends her days writing fantastical stories full of dark sexy vampires, hot shifters, sexy aliens, jaw-dropping demons, sinful angels, and magical witches – and while they can be snarky and swear a lot, they mean well and you'll grow to love them. Honestly.

When she's not in her writing cave she's usually playing the Sims, Civilizations or something similar, binge watching Netflix or upping the ante in the crazy cat lady stakes.

Read more from Jane Hinchey
www.janehinchey.com

CPSIA information can be obtained
at www.ICGtesting.com
Printed in the USA
LVOW12s0834090218
565936LV00001B/13/P